*For Dad and Gayle
and our unforgettable Costa Rica
adventures*

a **Four Seasons Park** sweet romantic comedy

JUST ONE SUMMER

WITH THE *Grumpy Boss*

SASHA HART

ONE

IT ALL STARTED with a fortune cookie.

I know, I know. It's a little piece of paper printed by some company that mass produces these things and comes up with fortunes that can apply to anyone, like "Something great is coming your way." Who doesn't have something great happen to them at least once in their life after reading that?

But when your life is a chain of odd coincidences that work out in your favor, you start to pay attention. Like the guy who found my lost phone at a restaurant and later became my boyfriend. (It only lasted a week, but I'll take good luck where I can get it.) Or the Help Wanted poster on the wall right after I saw my lucky number. That job turned out to be the highest-paying job yet—a receptionist position at billionaire Chase Everett's event management company and the perfect job for me.

So today, as I sat at my dining table eating cheap Chinese leftovers for breakfast before work, you'd better believe my breath caught as I stared at that tiny slip of paper surrounded by broken cookie pieces. It read, "Your future spouse will cross your path today."

Very specific. Almost oddly so.

If that wasn't enough, my online horoscope app's popup appeared minutes later, just as I arrived at the subway station for my work commute. Almost like the universe had coordinated it. I plopped onto the last subway seat and stared at the message, ignoring the wailing of a child across the car and the heavy body odor of the bearded man to my right.

"Your decisions today can bring the very lifelong romance you thought impossible—but you must become the pursuer."

I read it three times, chuckling as the subway started to pick up speed. I only found one love impossible—Ty, my ex. The one who not only got away, but hashed my heart to pieces in the process. And I'd let him do it. Just like I'd allowed myself to get laid off from two jobs and evicted from an apartment in the year since then. No, that particular lifelong romance wasn't very likely. Not that I even wanted that. Did I?

Nope. The only lifelong romance I really wanted right now was with whoever could pay my late rent and cancel out the eviction notice someone had slid into my mailbox last week. I had thirty days to figure this out or find a cheaper place, something I knew would be impossible. I'd been lucky enough to find this one and convince my roommates to ignore my poor credit history.

Fate and destiny had taken good care of me till now, but at some point, I'd have to figure things out for myself. Be the pursuer, like the horoscope said. Because leaving New York and going back home to Arkansas was *not* an option.

I let my finger hover over the message, hesitating, then took a screenshot of my horoscope before clearing it. I had to find a second job, and fast. The last thing I needed was a new relationship right now.

Sorry, Fate. Today isn't a good day for lifelong romance.

When the subway halted at my stop, I pushed through the crowd, avoiding the gaze of every man I passed just in case. I darted past wide smiles and sharply-dressed men on the wide sidewalks of Manhattan and made it to the office in record time.

When I entered the tall, shiny building with EVERETT EVENTS in block letters above the double glass doors and clocked in at the shiny front desk, I sent Dani a wave. The redhead took one look at me and muttered something about living in a junkyard.

A junkyard? I brushed my denim skirt and took a second look at my blouse, suddenly wishing I'd thought to iron it. The buttons didn't align correctly, leaving a button hanging by itself at the crook of my throat. Meanwhile, Dani looked like she'd walked right out of a shampoo commercial despite the five-hour shift she'd just finished. The woman's bright red hair hung perfectly straight over her shoulders as if nothing defied her will, even rain or gravity. She probably ironed and pressed her underwear and hung it up in the closet, all color-sorted. I didn't have to take a look in the mirror to know that my naturally curly hair would look wild and untamed in comparison.

Nevertheless, Dani looked the part of an Everett representative, and I very much did not. Which would only matter if Chase Everett walked in.

A *Hello, Daphne* from her would have been nice though.

The phone rang and rang and, not surprisingly, Dani ignored it completely. A stack of work still sat in the black bins on our shared reception desk. The same size as yesterday. Had she done anything at all?

I grabbed the phone behind Dani. "Everett Events. How can I help you?" There was only silence on the other end.

Dani sprinted from the desk to open the heavy glass door. "Mr. Everett. Nice to see you here today."

Chase Everett barely gave her a glance as he swept in the door, and I do mean *swept*. The guy swept everywhere he went. Not like a broom, but like a movie star. He definitely looked more Dani than Daphne, if you got my meaning. His broad shoulders filled his light blue shirt perfectly, and his tie hung perfectly centered in front of a hard, straight chest. A pair of expensive sunglasses covered eyes I'd never seen in person. The guy probably wore sunglasses at midnight.

And the swagger. Oh, wow. It was like he knew he was New York's most eligible bachelor and wanted to leave every woman's jaw hanging in his wake.

"Tell Blythe to meet me in my office," he grumbled to me, heading for the elevator without sending me a glance or bothering to reply to Dani's greeting. In fact, he seemed unaware of her presence at all.

A dial tone sounded in my ear. "Yes, sir," I managed, hanging up the phone.

He strode into the elevator the second the doors opened. I found myself holding my breath as the doors closed, and the lobby and the world around us returned to normal.

"Jerk," Dani muttered, still holding the door. Then she slipped through the doorway and disappeared into the hustle of downtown Manhattan.

I knew all about self-made billionaire Mr. Everett, at least the parts other employees of Everett Events were willing to share. The man barely spoke, hardly ever looked you in the eye, and wanted absolute perfection. He resented being argued with and expected instant obedience. How I'd even gotten this job, I didn't know. Desperation on the part of Blythe, my manager and the resident wedding planner? She'd thrown a lot of work at me the moment she hired me on, probably because

Dani refused to do anything she deemed grunt work. Which meant pretty much everything but answering the phone and batting her eyelashes at the grooms who came to meet with their wedding planner.

Despite being here nearly six months, I still got the feeling Chase Everett didn't know my name.

But hey, at least he'd talked to me today, even if it was an order.

I hit the appropriate button on the phone, relayed the message to my boss, and grimaced again at the state of my blouse. I'd been off by not one button, but *two*. I looked like a first-grader playing dress-up. At least Chase hadn't seemed to notice my clothing malfunction. There were no clients currently in the lobby—I'd hurry and fix that right now. Knowing my luck, Chase would choose today, of all days, to actually look at me on his way out. Getting fired would not help the whole eviction problem at home.

Maybe if I gave my loft to someone else and took the couch...but no. Absolutely not. I would not be the only working twenty-six-year-old woman in New York sleeping on a flea-infested sofa. There had to be better options than that.

I finished with the top button and started on the second, taking a seat to avoid direct eye contact with anyone walking by outside. The lobby felt like working in a fishbowl sometimes. The windows were tinted so it was difficult for people to see inside, but I could see far more of the outdoors than I wanted to these days—including a man walking around in a Speedo and nothing else, women dragging toilet paper along under their high heels, and gusts of wind causing the occasional shirt or skirt to fly skyward. As awkward as my particular wardrobe malfunction was today, at least I had somewhere to hide in order to fix it.

The third button. This would be the most awkward, fixing

the bulge right above my breasts. From the side, my bra would be visible.

Nobody come in, nobody come in, I pleaded with the universe, keeping my ears tuned for the sound of the door opening to a new client. But the city noise remained firmly locked away.

The elevator dinged. Someone had arrived in the lobby.

My finger slipped, forcing me to start over. I would conquer this stupid button yet. It would not win—

"Daphne?"

The sound of my ex-boyfriend's voice sent a wave of horror through me.

But no, that couldn't be right. I hadn't seen him in nearly a year. My visitor had to have a similar voice. Because of all the hundreds of thousands of people in Manhattan, the chances of Ty showing up here while I hid, half-clothed, one hand covering my oddly bulging shirt, would be astronomical.

I slowly turned in my chair to find Ty standing behind the counter, looking down at me.

His beautiful eyes slid down to my hand and back up to my face. "It is you. Your hair is different, but I thought..." He seemed to get a hold of himself and grinned. "What are you doing?"

"I, um. Just a second." I turned away and hurriedly fastened the rest of the buttons, the heat from my face practically heating the air all around me. Then I swept a hand over my unruly hair and turned, hoping I looked poised and confident. "I had a button issue, but it's taken care of now."

"Ah. So you ducked back there to fix it." His gaze slid to my blouse again and back to my face. "You don't actually work here...?"

That night almost a year ago came flooding back—my tears as I'd fled his apartment after he dumped me. Ty, an attorney himself, had accused me of floating along in the fast-paced river of New York commerce without a single career goal to my name. Definitely *not* true. I was just between dreams at the moment.

But if he found out I worked here, a part-time receptionist at a very temporary dead-end desk job, it would only prove him right.

"No, no," I said quickly, grateful I didn't have a name tag. "I'm actually just here to...meet someone. But there's no receptionist right now."

The lie settled in my gut, but staring at the man who'd been my real dream and my everything for nearly two years and the longest relationship of my life, I didn't regret it one bit.

That seemed to satisfy him. "Makes sense. I've only ever come in the morning when Dani was here. Maybe they don't have an afternoon receptionist. Is your meeting with Blythe? She had to end our appointment early because she got called in to something, but I bet you can find her business card here somewhere." He searched the desk, found the card holder with Blythe's contact information, and handed me one.

"Thanks." Time for this conversation to end, and fast. If another client walked in, I couldn't keep pretending I didn't work here. I'd lose my job.

Wait. *Another* client. There was only one reason Ty would meet with Blythe. "Are you getting married?" *Please say no.*

He nodded. "Yes. Destination wedding. It's all happened so fast, but her parents are paying, and everything sort of fell into place." His gaze dropped to my very ring-less hand. "Is that why you're here too?"

Destination wedding. Her parents are paying. His fiancée had to be loaded indeed. Everett only planned events for the most elite clients in Manhattan—the snobbish Chase Everett crowd. What female eyes could Ty have drawn long enough to get them engaged so soon after his last relationship?

"It isn't official yet," I said casually, hoping he couldn't see my mind racing. "But we're talking about it. We have our sights on a little island off the coast of Costa Rica called Isle de Pura Vida." Everett Events hosted almost exclusively there, so hopefully he would buy it.

"Same!" he exclaimed. "Wouldn't that be ironic, both of us getting married on the same tiny island? And using the same wedding planner too, in a city as big as New York."

I forced a chuckle. What if he was only pretending to go along with my lie and secretly laughed at my poor attempt at self-preservation?

Or worse. What if, at this moment, he was questioning his marriage plans and my own relationship status drove him to go through with it anyway?

A realization slapped me right in the stunned brain. *The fortune cookie. The horoscope.* This had to be the relationship they referred to. Ty and I could still be meant for each other.

My destiny stood right in front of me.

"Very ironic," I finally agreed. "Your fiancée must have some money to afford Everett." Ty had been a junior attorney at a huge firm downtown, so unless something had drastically changed in the last year, he'd be relying on her wealth for a long while.

"She does. Her family owns a hotel chain, so they're putting up the entire wedding party on the island. According to the tabloids, it'll be the event of the season."

There it was again—the slightest note of disappointment. Resignation, even. Could it be that he regretted his engagement? Was he harboring second thoughts? Were any of those second thoughts about me?

"And you?" he asked after a long silence, seeming reluctant

to end the conversation quite yet. "Unless you've won the lottery since the last time I saw you, your boyfriend must have some serious wealth."

I nodded, my cheeks heating again. He knew about my rocky past when it came to employment. I'd only managed one year of college before fleeing my Arkansas hometown, and my livestock and harvesting skills weren't exactly appreciated here. Why was New York so blasted expensive?

I couldn't think of a profession that would justify being a client here, so I merely said, "He does very well for himself."

"Secretive as ever," Ty said. "Mystery Man is a lucky guy."

I felt an almost overwhelming urge to scream at him. Couldn't he see that my life had only fallen apart since that awful night? How could he go and marry another when something clearly still existed between us? Even now, his eyes held mine with a certainty that hooked me like a fish on a line.

Still there. All the magic from before, all the fate and meaning...

Ty was supposed to be mine. I had no doubt of that now. We were supposed to meet here, the two of us, and get back together.

Only one thing stood in our way—the tiny little matter of his destination wedding.

Ty seemed resigned, but it wasn't over till the rings exchanged hands and the pastor said, "I now pronounce you husband and wife." I just had to stop the event from happening. Was that what the horoscope meant by becoming the pursuer?

"Well, it was good to run into you again. I hope your wedding goes well." He turned toward the door.

No, no, no. "Ty, wait—"

The elevator doors opened and a stream of curses arose from the woman inside. My wedding planner boss, Blythe, stormed out and practically sprinted for the doors, her arms full of belongings, her purse dragging along behind her. A trail of papers followed, and she didn't seem to care, shoving through the glass doors as if driven out by a fire. Before I knew it, she was gone.

Ty and I looked at each other in confusion. What in the world?

"Daphne," a male voice said from the elevator.

We both turned to find Chase Everett standing inside, his eyes fixed on me. His gaze sent a jolt of live electricity up and down my limbs, and I was suddenly very aware of my appearance.

Then I realized what this looked like—that Chase was my boyfriend, and my entire body warmed at the very thought. Me and the most eligible bachelor in New York. I mean, I could definitely do worse. If I meant to make Ty jealous out of his mind, that would do it. *No goals, indeed,* I wanted to spit back at him.

Instead, I smiled sweetly at my ex. "It was good to see you too. If you'll excuse me."

As I took my place next to Chase Everett—*the* Chase Everett—in the elevator, I watched as Ty stared at me, a stunned expression on his face, until the doors closed between us.

TWO

"Was that a client?" Chase asked as the seconds passed. His voice sounded odd in here. Too loud and a little echo-y.

"Yes." My voice was clipped, and I couldn't help it. Thanks to Chase, I didn't know if I'd ever see Ty again. I'd deleted his number from my phone a long time ago, and surely he'd blocked me on social media. I doubted the guy still lived in his dumpy apartment if he was engaged to some hotel chain heiress. That meant I'd either have to hunt down his number in company records or rely solely on fate to bring us back together. But what if that encounter downstairs was it, my one chance? If I never saw Ty again, I'd wonder what might have happened for the rest of my life.

All because of a stern billionaire boss who wanted to meet with me at the worst possible moment . . . who also happened to smell really, *really* good.

I recalled Blythe storming out and realized what all this meant. Had he fired her?

Was I next?

The doors finally opened, and Chase waited for me to step

out. I'd expected another lobby and perhaps a personal assistant, but no. There were only tall windows, bright white furniture, tall grasses in standing vases, and string music blaring from a speaker in the wall. A glass desk sat next to a far window, its contents neatly organized. The entire floor had to be this guy's office.

Chase motioned to one of the chairs. "Have a seat."

I thought of Ty downstairs. He couldn't have gotten far. "If you're firing me, I'd rather you do it now so I can gather my things."

He blinked. "Why would I fire you?"

"I mean, not that I want you to," I said, hedging my words now. "Didn't you just fire Blythe?"

"Of course. I would have done it last month, but it took a while to get the proof together. Embezzlement is a serious crime, and she made a pretty devastating dent before I discovered her activities. I like evidence that can't be refuted." He tipped his head toward the window overlooking the street. "Like that Ferrari parked on the side of the road."

I let that sink in before stepping to the glass and looking down. Indeed, Blythe was shoving her belongings into the passenger side. She slammed the door, rounded the vehicle, and nearly got herself hit by a bicycle in the bike lane as she climbed into the driver's seat. She seemed to shout something after the biker before closing her door and pulling into traffic.

"Maybe she saved up for it," I said slowly, unsure why I was even defending her. "Or has a massive car payment. She's married—her husband could be paying for it."

"Her husband is living in Wyoming with his girlfriend. That's why it took so long to confirm our suspicions. I had to make sure this wasn't a revenge purchase. However, I'd appreciate your keeping that secret until the court proceedings are finished." Chase motioned back to the chair, a note of irritation in his voice. "Shall we?"

Far below, Ty emerged onto the street. He stared back inside the building for a few seconds, then lifted his gaze as if he felt me watching him. I sensed the wistfulness in that gaze. It wasn't the expression of a man in love with someone else. So why was he marrying this woman?

Seconds later, he strode down the sidewalk and out of sight.

Chase's gaze could have burned a hole in my back. I squared my shoulders and practically marched to the chair he'd indicated, plopping into it. Then I pasted on my fakest of professional smiles. "What can I do for you?"

Chase sat across from me, completely missing my own irritation. "Blythe said you were the more competent of the two assistants. I need you to help sort through her mess, figure out what still needs to be done and when. As you know, Everett Events hosts only the most exclusive of celebrity weddings, and we try to keep those centralized on Isle de Pura Vida so they have the very best experience possible. We have six events left before the rainy season begins, and the next is this weekend. Blythe chose the worst possible time to pull this. I'll have to hire someone skilled to replace her as our wedding coordinator, and fast."

An idea sprang to mind. An idea so clever and delicious, it almost felt like fate. Like a horoscope prediction coming true, perhaps.

Suddenly I knew exactly how to get Ty back.

"Nobody else can get trained in time," I told him. "You need someone who knows the business and has met the clients. Someone who works with all our vendors on a daily basis and solves problems almost before they occur. Someone hands-on."

He leaned back in his ridiculously white chair, and despite being inside, he wore his usual sunglasses. Even with dark glass covering his eyes, I spotted eyes darker than a bay stallion. "You," he said. His perfect lips curved slightly.

I couldn't tell whether he seemed pleased or amused. "The very same."

"You've been here what, six months?"

I blinked in surprise. "Almost exactly, yes."

He rested an ankle on his opposite knee, the most casual pose I'd ever seen him use. "We have people with decades of experience. What makes you think you'd do a better job than any of them?"

"Because I've been doing Blythe's job all along," I said, surprised at the confidence in my tone. *Pursuer vibes.* "She only came into the office to meet with clients. She showed them books that I compiled and wrote out a list that she then gave to me to fulfill before leaving again. I assure you, the company will be in good hands with me in charge. I know that, because they're the same hands that have kept it running for months."

Chase dropped his leg and leaned forward. "This will be an on-site position on Isle de Pura Vida. Blythe liked to travel back and forth, but we'd have you stay there for the last few weeks of the dry season until our last event is over. You'd be dealing directly with clients and ensuring everything goes smoothly. It's very different from placing orders and taking calls."

Working on an island for the summer. The island where Ty would be arriving very soon. It felt like an entire vat of chocolate fudge ice cream, there for the taking.

I shrugged. "It can't be that different. Clients want a seamless experience, so we give that to them, no matter what it takes. I know how to operate in the background." If there was one thing I could do well, it was be invisible. Or at least, I'd assumed so until Chase Everett summoned me into his office. Suite. Whatever.

"Perhaps. But do you know how to operate in the foreground? These are multi-million-dollar clients. Every detail has to be perfect. Even..." He motioned to my blouse.

I looked down to find my blouse's buttons corrected, but a wide sweet-and-sour-chicken stain now front and center.

My face heated, but I drew up straight, trying my best to look confident and unaffected. "I'm exactly what you're looking for. You have my word that everything will go smoothly with me in charge."

Please say yes. Please say yes.

Chase examined me for a long moment, then cocked his head. "Well, then, Daphne Porter. You'd better get packed, because your plane to paradise leaves tonight."

♥ ♥ ♥ ♥ ♥

When I got back to my apartment, I picked my way through the clutter of the living room that served as my roommate's bedroom and up the metal steps to the loft. At least, that's what real estate sites called it—this tiny corner of the apartment had no walls or privacy and even less space. I could cross the entire thing in four big steps and slept in a full-sized bed, not even a queen, and I hadn't been able to scrub away the wet dog smell from its previous inhabitant. Nevertheless, it was mine, and I paid dearly for it with each month's rental payment.

Or rather, I had until last month, when I'd been forced to choose between rent and groceries. If only my job paid better than a high-school student's salary. Maybe that would change now, with this huge promotion.

Unless I managed to steal Ty back, which meant saying goodbye to Everett Events and its paychecks for good.

The thought made me a little sad. I'd finally found a job I was good at. Surely winning Ty would be worth the sacrifice.

I sat on the left side of the bed to avoid the sunken right and whipped out my phone.

Bridget answered on the first ring. "What do you have to say for yourself?"

Taken aback, I tried to remember our last conversation. Texting, a week ago. I think. "I'm...not sure. What do *you* think I have to say for myself?"

"I knew it. You completely forgot."

Crap. What had I forgotten? "Uh..."

"Your parents' anniversary is kind of a big deal. You could have at least sent them a text."

Right. My parents' anniversary yesterday. "Wait, how do you even know when that is?"

"Doc Shore baked them a pie and boasted all over town about it. I swear the man only did it to brag about his baking skills to Patti Wilkins, but she didn't even give him a second glance. Meanwhile, Carlie decided to make a cake because that's bigger than a pie, so of course Ms. Phillips made her four-layer chocolate death cake to show them all up. Needless to say, your parents could start a bakery with the sweets sitting in their kitchen."

Our neighbors had spent hours making my folk's day special, whatever their reasons, and I hadn't even sent a text. Mom would be crushed. "Dad doesn't even eat sweets."

"I told them that, but nobody listens to me." My friend sighed. "I think the only way to apologize for an oversight this big is to come home and pay them a visit."

"And by extension, you."

"Naturally."

I groaned. "This is where I remind you that I haven't been home in almost seven years."

"And this is where I remind you that your parents miss you, and so does Rosie. Horses don't live forever, you know."

By that, I knew she was referring to my parents. But Bridget would never say such a thing aloud, not after Dad's bout with cancer. She didn't realize it, but I called the doctor twice a year for updates about his condition. Dad would never tell me anything. I knew that from painful experience.

I would never tell him so, but I often lit candles for him at churches, even though I rarely attended. I even avoided walking under ladders or breaking glass, just in case. If I were to see any black cats crossing my path, I would have avoided them too. Anything to feel like I was contributing to his health and well-being.

Anything except giving up and going home.

"Don't you think it's time to reconcile?" Bridget asked, her voice softening. "I'm sure they're sorry about what they did."

I wasn't sure at all. Dad only seemed to get more proud as the years went on, and I was my father's daughter. Talking about that awful day was the last thing I wanted to do right now, though, so I forced lightness into my voice. "Thanks for the reminder. I'll send them a 'Happy Anniversary' e-card with lots of emojis."

"Don't make me come down there," Bridget growled.

I grinned at that. "I thought you'd never offer." Her last visit had been over the week of Christmas, and we'd somehow managed to squish into my tiny loft for most of her stay. It didn't quite feel like the old high school days when we'd raced our horses in muddy fields and had sleepovers full of giggling gossip and elaborate future plans involving boys whose names I couldn't even remember. While my parents had lectured me about my astrology obsession, Bridget had bought me a magic-8 ball for my sixteenth birthday. I'd brought it with me to New York.

"Not a chance," Bridget objected. "It's your turn to come here this time. You owe me. Have you ever had to drive an old truck through the streets of New York at Christmastime, looking for parking that doesn't exist?"

I had to admit I hadn't. I knew better than to own a car here, not that I could have afforded one anyway. "That does sound terrible. How about I make you a seven-layer chocolate cake to rival Ms. Phillips'?"

"And then you'll make me come there to get it."

"Exactly."

We both laughed, the years melting away as we did. Bridget had visited me at least once a year since I'd left, always bringing baked goodies from Mom and sometimes wrapped gifts as well. In my defense, I always sent her back with gifts too—usually three for each of my parents to cover Christmas, Mother's or Father's Day, and their birthdays. Mom kept the gifts in her closet until it was time to open them and gushed about each one over the phone, pretending nothing at all was amiss. Dad always refused to come to the phone, feigning exhaustion or conveniently being gone when I called on holidays. Ours was a stubborn standoff that neither would stoop low enough to end.

"Actually," I began, "I know you were planning to come in a few weeks, but I need to take a raincheck. Something has come up." I plugged in my laptop, pulled up my streaming service, and turned on the movie I'd started last night. Cavil's gritty voice started blaring in the middle of an argument; he looked handsome even in black-and-white with his cowboy hat and leather chaps.

She snorted. "You're watching it again, aren't you?"

"Watching what?"

"What do you think? *The* movie. You could act out every part by memory. In your sleep and upside down and across the world, with your hands tied."

"Come on. That's unfair." I paused. "Most of the parts I couldn't act out properly with my hands tied."

"Daphne."

"All right, fine. I watched most of it last night, and I was going to finish tonight, and I will not be judged by you."

"Just because you're in love with a man old enough to be your great-great-great grandfather."

"Not so! You have to be alive to be old. He died like forty years ago."

"My point exactly. I must insist that you start dating real men. As in, men who exist in this decade. Preferably ones who don't go around shooting their enemies. You live in New York, for goodness sake. There must be a million single guys there."

"But they don't go galloping after trains to win back the beautiful maiden, now, do they? Okay, you're right. I'll call my mom and wish her a happy anniversary, and I won't fawn over men I can't have."

She paused. "Well, you can fawn over certain men you can't have. Just make sure they're alive first. I mean, you work for Chase freaking Everett. Do you see him every day?"

I thought for a second. "No. He's usually up in his office before my afternoon shift starts and he stays late. But occasionally." Not that he'd ever paid me any heed until today.

"Has he ever spoken to you? Like, said your name? I think I would die if he said my name." Her voice lowered. "*Bridget, you were meant to be mine. Marry me.*"

And she said *I* was the pathetic one. I took a deep breath. "Actually, he pulled me into his office today."

"Really???"

I glared at my laptop. "Bridget, I swear. Get your mind out of the gutter. He offered me a promotion, that's all."

"Oh. Well, that's good. Very exciting." She paused. "But

you were alone with him for how long? I bet something *could have* happened if you'd let it."

"Anyway," I said, pulling her back to the point. "You're talking to the new on-site event coordinator. I'm flying out to Isle de Pura Vida tonight."

"You're moving to Chase Everett's private island?" She sounded breathless now.

"Yes, but only for the summer. But here's the best part." I told her about Ty and running into him today, leaving out the wayward blouse part and other awkward details. By the time I finished, my chattering friend was stunned speechless.

"A fortune cookie *and* a horoscope," she said. "That's, like, a done deal. Guaranteed. You guys are supposed to be together, end of story."

"Well, I'm not sure he'll see it that way considering he's marrying Veronica Loyal in a few weeks." I'd looked him up after my meeting with Chase and nearly fell over at his fiancée's name. The woman had starred on a reality TV show, for goodness' sake. A model. She appeared on the list of wealthiest women in the world. Her and Ty? It made no sense. I only had to prove that to him.

"Veronica Loyal," Bridget breathed. "Right."

"Don't worry though. I have a plan. I just have to keep my job long enough for Ty to arrive, and then I'll help him see things my way."

"But…" My friend hesitated for a long moment. "If you steal the groom, Chase will have to fire you."

"Chase won't even notice. He's too busy spending his millions to worry about managing the day-to-day affairs of his company in an opposite hemisphere."

"Billions, Daphne. He's a billionaire. Way bigger than millions."

"I realize that, but it doesn't change fate."

"Right, okay. Setting our sights on Ty. Yes, I'll wait to visit you until the fall when you're home. Assuming you aren't getting married before then, and you darn well better invite me. I stayed to help Pops with his dementia, but that doesn't mean I can't leave for important stuff like this."

"Invite you? You'll be planning it, maid of honor. We both know you're the real wedding planner here."

"The bitter irony," she said with a sigh. "Fine, it's a deal. But you'd better call me every day. I have nothing else to do out here in boonie-ville but live vicariously through you."

THREE

S<small>UNSHINE</small>—<small>CHECK</small>.

Floppy hat—check.

Sunscreen—check.

I glanced backward at the enormous resort, all bright and expensive and *everything,* and felt my smile widen. Tropical paradise—check.

Grateful I'd gotten a pedicure before my flight, I slid my foot out of its sandal and dipped my toe into the pool water. Then I groaned. Perfect. I could spend all day every day out here.

And I would be getting paid to do it.

Okay, so I wasn't a resort guest. Not officially. But since Chase also owned the resort, we were allowed to use the grounds when dressed as guests. My tiny bungalow—a *bunga-low!*—was only a quarter of a mile inland. Not quite close enough to see the beach, but still close enough to smell it. Taste it. Feel it on the wind.

This was too good to be true. Blue skies, a green rainforest all around us, the perfect temperature, the warm sun on my skin, a slight breeze, soft sand beaches . . . and Ty in my future.

"I was born for this," I muttered, pulling my foot back onto the heated deck. I would take a dip later. Right now, all I wanted to do was lounge. Not because I was stereotypical or anything, but simply because I could.

And because tomorrow would be my first official day on the job, and I had no idea what I'd gotten myself into.

A raised voice floated over the pool. Two men stood across the deck, arguing. The shorter of the two moved his hands in an animated fashion, looking defensive. The taller shook his head slowly, as if in disapproval. The taller one looked slightly familiar.

I blinked. It couldn't be. Could it?

The man must have felt my gaze, because he turned in my direction. That confirmed it—Chase Everett, all six feet four inches of him. He wore a black T-shirt that clung to his frame in an unusually casual way, and his hair blew slightly in the breeze.

What was he doing here? I thought he'd sent me here to handle things on his behalf. Didn't he trust that I could do the job?

Then his eyes narrowed, and I realized I was staring at him like a fool. I found a lounge chair, mentally kicking myself for the sudden heat in my cheeks. I had just as much of a right to be poolside as he did.

The shorter man barked a laugh, loud and bitter. Then he shook his head and stormed away. Chase watched him go with a strange expression on his face. Disappointment?

Seconds later, Chase disappeared into one of the resort buildings.

The man who'd argued with him emerged from the pool-house, slammed a door, and swept toward me in a torrent of anger, muttering to himself.

Just before he passed, I leaned forward. "Difficult boss?"

He paused and released a frustrated breath. "I cannot say." The man's voice was slightly accented.

"You can say whatever you want to me. Chase is my boss too." I gave him an understanding grin.

"You are the new wedding planner." He stuck out a friendly hand, his entire demeanor suddenly welcoming. I took it and we shook hands. "I hope you last longer than the previous two. They had no chance. I don't think Chase really wanted them to succeed."

I cocked an eyebrow. "Why?"

"He's a billionaire. He owns the entire island. What's a worker or two to him?"

I remembered the way Chase's eyes always passed over me when he walked through the office foyer. I'd been surprised to find he knew my name, because I couldn't remember a single time he'd actually seen me. "I know what you mean."

He leaned in and lowered his voice. I smelled alcohol on his breath. "However, Chase may not be in charge much longer. Then all will be well. Much easier when that day comes."

I frowned, unsure what he meant by that. "Why would he not be in charge?" The man owned the island, Everett Events, and the resort itself. Was he selling soon?

The pool man's mouth quirked. "Just be careful, wedding planner. Stay far away from Chase Everett, or he will take you down with him."

❤ ❤ ❤ ❤ ❤

"The airport was so dirty," said the woman on the phone. "And the tiny roads? Atrocious. When your company said this would be a tropical paradise getaway, I was stupid enough to believe it. You really need to work on your advertising." She paused. "I'm so embarrassed that Kevin Franklin is coming."

I had no idea who Kevin Franklin was, but I could tell she expected me to be impressed. "I'm sorry to hear you haven't been enjoying your stay so far, Ms. Holland." I fingered the list I'd been making—the plan to get Ty back. This simple piece of paper would change my life and ensure my future with the man I loved, yet here I stood, taking bridezilla calls while work piled up around me.

"How can I enjoy it when there's nothing to do?" she moaned. "My fiancé is out there scuba diving, but I'm not certified. Sunbathing would risk my perfect tan. Even snorkeling would give me that weird tan line, you know, the ugly one on your neck and the back of your arms? No thanks."

My mind whirled. I was a wedding planner, not her vacation planner. Had Blythe dealt with clients like this?

Kamia Holland, I reminded myself. This woman would soon become a multi-millionaire. She could squash me in her sleep. I imagined her in that beautiful penthouse, staring at the view she would only enjoy through glass and the ocean she wouldn't touch, and tried to see this incredible paradise from her perspective.

"Of course," I said evenly. "Snorkeling isn't a great pre-wedding activity anyway. I do have a few ideas though. I'll be sending you a little gift in a few minutes. Will you still be in your room?"

"Where else would I be?" the woman snapped.

Outside, on one of the most beautiful islands on Earth. But I was too smart to say that aloud, instead falling on the three lines I'd learned working at the Greek restaurant last year. "Thanks so much for letting me know about your experience. Your feedback is always appreciated. We're grateful for your business."

"I should say so." My phone beeped. She'd hung up.

I gritted my teeth and shoved the phone back into my pocket. It bulged—too big. I hated large phones and too-small pockets. Why couldn't there be man-sized pockets in everything? It wouldn't solve my bridezilla problem, but it couldn't hurt either.

With a sigh, I gestured to the assistant across the room. The man scurried over. I'd expected my office to at least have four walls, but no. I worked in a rented building with an open wall facing the hotels lining the beach. Granted, those elements were pretty tame and the view...well, pretty, if not of the beach itself. Most of the island was covered in lush greenery, and the resort was no exception. But the fresh air felt distracting at times. I found it hard to sit at a desk with paradise just outside the door. Er, wall.

"Yes?" my assistant asked. I kept forgetting his name as he didn't wear a name tag, but the clean-shaven dark-skinned man with tightly shorn black hair always wore a smile. I'd liked him immediately.

"I need a gift basket, preferably with gift cards. Big ones. What ideas do you have?"

He cocked his head. "Gift cards?"

That's right. Island. "Um, salon...money? Prepaid?" The second I said it, I knew Kamia would never set foot in a salon here. Not when she'd paid thousands of primping dollars in New York before coming here. She'd insist they would ruin her perfect finishes. "Actually, never mind. How about food? Are there healthy food places around here?" Food always made people feel better...unless they were on a wedding diet, which Kamia likely was. The woman probably survived on straight lettuce and pills these days. "Nope. Won't work either."

My assistant—I really needed to write down his name—smiled again, making me instantly jealous of his straight white teeth. "It's okay. You are dealing with hard client, yes?"

"Very."

"She need massage. All ladies need. I know American masseuse, very expensive. I will arrange immediately. You want basket, I will make."

I'd forgotten. This guy had worked under every wedding planner since Chase founded the company. He had way more experience taming unruly bridezillas than I did. "Thank you. Can you make it—"

"Pretty?" He grinned again, knowingly this time. "Yes, miss. I know the person who make ones for other planners. It will be perfect."

"You're saving me. I really appreciate it." I hoped Chase paid the guy well. Probably not half as well as he deserved.

As he left, I remembered Chase's run-in with that worker yesterday at the pool. Apparently, his reputation of being hard on employees wasn't too far off. But what had the guy meant when he said Chase wouldn't be in charge much longer? Such an odd thing to say about the owner of a corporation. And why was Chase here in the first place?

Focus, I ordered myself, turning back to the sheet of paper in front of me that read BATTLE PLAN in bold letters. If I took this step by step, Ty would be mine by the end of the month.

I wrote a few ideas, complete with bullet points, and felt a swell of excitement inside. I was really going to do this. I, Daphne Porter, had finally begun to chase my future like a cowboy chasing a train. I could claim what the universe told me was mine.

"See you, Agwe," Chase called in the distance.

Chase.

I leaped to my feet and hid the Battle Plan, straightening a stack of papers over it before remembering I would look busier with a messy desk. I brushed a few pages off and accidentally scattered the entire stack just as Chase stepped inside.

One of the papers went flying toward him, arched upward, and then sank slowly to the floor at his feet.

He eyed it in confusion, then picked it up. "Battle plan?"

With a squeak, I hurried around the desk and swiped it from his hands. "It's just what I call my to-do list," I lied. "Sounds more fun that way."

Chase stared at me. "Do you always have 'Find out where he's staying' on your to-do list?"

Crap. At least I hadn't used Ty's name. "Oh, that's just a client. A groom. Husband-to-be. But not mine, obviously. I wanted to make sure his accommodations were acceptable. He has very high expectations."

Amusement entered Chase's eyes, though it didn't quite reach his mouth. *Those lips.* So perfect. "All our clients stay at the resort, the one associated with the company. It's part of their package. You didn't know that?"

"No, no, I did," I said quickly, feeling my face flush again. Why did it do that at the worst possible times? "It's just that he...also rented a place on the island to give him and his bride a little more privacy for the honeymoon. Not all couples like hotels." That sounded plausible, right? If anything, it seemed like something Ty would do.

"Hmm." He seemed to buy it, pressing his lips together thoughtfully. "I wonder if we should offer that option in the package. When you find out the location of the suite, let me know. We'll see if it's in the budget."

I hadn't known there *was* a budget for multi-million-dollar weddings, and that seemed like something the wedding planner should know, but I just nodded. "Of course. How long are you in town?"

"For the foreseeable future. The VP of finance is handling things in New York, so I'll take the island shift. Make sure everything goes smoothly. We can't have any mistakes." His stare felt heavier than an elephant on my head.

An elephant on my head? This wasn't a time for my brain to go kaput. Sure, Chase was attractive, but I wasn't one of those fumbling females who swooned whenever an attractive billionaire bachelor walked by—especially one who also happened to be my boss and who held my entire livelihood and future in his hands.

Mostly.

I drew myself together and tried to look every inch the poised, professional employee he expected. "I know how important this is, and I assure you, I have everything under control. Your clients are in good hands."

"I've heard that before. Almost word-for-word, actually. Let's hope you're the first to really mean it." Chase started to turn away, then stopped. "Welcome to Isle de Pura Vida, Daphne Porter. I hope you enjoy your stay."

FOUR

I wish I could say the day got better, but it didn't. The shipment of chicken thighs from the States had turned out to have bones in them, which bridezilla—er, Kamia—had specifically condemned. Company policy stated the meat had to go through a specific sterilization process that didn't exist here or on any of the nearby islands or the closest mainland, not that they even raised chickens here in the quantities we would need. It meant we'd either have to separate the meat from the bone ourselves at a substantial increase of cost in labor, which Chase would insist wasn't in the budget, or inform the couple they'd be serving chicken thighs with—heaven forbid—actual bones.

The choice was easy. I spent all night in the kitchens, separating the meat myself. A few workers felt sorry for me and stayed to help, but even then, I stumbled back to my room at 5:00 a.m., completely exhausted and smelling like a butcher.

When I finally made it into the office just past nine, nursing a headache, a yellow sticky note waited on my stack of papers which, thankfully, no longer held my battle plan as I'd moved

that to the security of my phone. I didn't recognize the scrib-
bled handwriting.

> *It's after 8 and you aren't here. I need a
> list of the excursions booked for our clients this
> week right away. I also want you to participate in
> several to get a feel for what we offer. Here are
> a few pamphlets. Maybe offer to take Kamia on
> one later today. She's been complaining to every
> staff member she can find. —Chase*

Double crap. Of all the mornings for him to come by on
time. I stabbed the power button on the computer at my desk,
which was surely from the 90s because why would they have
updated technology in a multi-million-dollar corporation?

It took forever to load up. When it finally did, I grabbed the
file and put the information together as quickly as possible, my
fingers fumbling and my eyes burning from lack of sleep.

The last two names on the list made me stop.

Ty Symas and Veronica Loyal.

Seeing it in writing, all official, made my heart squeeze. I'd
seen his name with mine so many times, it felt like betrayal to
have it next to anyone else's.

Good thing I'm here then, I reminded myself. I wasn't here
to please Chase. As much as I appreciated the pay increase and
the tropical paradise, I didn't intend to stay forever. This was
only a step up to my real role in life—Mrs. Symas. That had to
remain the focus.

I took my finger off the track pad and left the names as they
were. A quick copy and paste, and Chase had the list.

*I also want you to participate in a few to get a feel for what
we offer.* At least that sounded like he expected me to stay.

With Chase watching my every move, fulfilling his request to entertain Kamia would best be done quickly. As tired as I was, a nap would have to wait.

I scanned the list, my eyes falling on the word "kayaking." That didn't seem too hard for a bride like Kamia, at least compared to the nature tour that required miles of hiking through a humid rainforest. And it would only take three hours, after which I could return home and crash without Chase judging my work ethic. Perfect.

I clicked on the excursion, used the company code to add myself to the list, and took a sip of the tea I'd grabbed this morning since there was no coffee.

It would be a long day.

♥ ♥ ♥ ♥ ♥

I pulled the ugly orange life jacket around my chest and fastened it closed, wincing at the wetness that immediately soaked through my shirt. I'd opted for a light T-shirt, bermuda shorts, and sandals given the circumstances, and was immediately glad for it. Every kayak had at least an inch of water at the bottom and the seats weren't much better.

"I have to sit in a puddle?" Kamia moaned next to me. She'd worn a pair of cropped white pants and a pink halter top.

"Better than swimming," a tall tourist said with a laugh.

Kamia turned and her eyes widened. I could almost hear harp music and angels singing in the background.

"True," she said softly.

He winked.

Oh, boy.

"Here, Kamia," I said, brushing the water off the seat. "Your shoes will get wet, but at least your pants won't." At least not until we got going. I'd been kayaking a dozen times. If she expected to stay completely dry, this would be a long afternoon.

She ignored me and the still-damp life jacket at her feet. "I'm Kamia, from Santa Monica. And you are?"

"Afonso from Portugal. Very pleased to meet you, Kamia." The model—er, tourist—inclined his head, which practically sent Kamia all aflutter.

I could see the light in her eyes, the excitement buzzing through her limbs. It's how I'd felt upon meeting Ty for the first time. It was also the last thing we needed right now.

"We'd better get going," I told Kamia, scooping up her life jacket and lifting it around her arms. "The tour guide is way ahead of us."

"Do you have a kayak partner, Afonso?" Kamia asked sweetly. "If not, I volunteer. I've always wanted to go to Portugal. Maybe you can tell me about it."

"Actually, Afonso is paired with me." Chase appeared from behind us, his life jacket hanging unclipped. He turned to the man. "You ready to go?"

Of course Chase would be here. I felt relieved and frustrated all at once. At least I wouldn't have to deal with Kamia alone, but why did Chase feel it necessary to stalk us? Didn't he trust me?

Afonso nodded reluctantly. "Yes, Chase Everett. I would be pleased to share a kayak with you."

Kamia grumbled a curse and took her seat.

Crisis averted. Maybe.

I forced Chase out of my mind and settled into a steady rhythm at first, grateful for the physical exertion after so long at a desk. My triceps began to burn, but in a good way. I would be delightfully sore tomorrow. How I missed the high school volleyball days, when every sport had come easily.

"You're going too fast," Kamia complained. "What is this, the Olympics?"

I shot a glance back at Chase and Afonso, who paddled in tandem slightly behind us. The farther ahead we got, the better. "I can't wait to show you Black Sand Beach. It's really something." I had no idea whether that was true, but it sounded like something a wedding planner would say.

"A beach full of volcanic gravel. Ooh, yay. Sounds like a winner."

To her credit, she didn't stop paddling and increased her pace. Probably so she didn't look weak in front of Afonso.

Every few minutes, I stole a glance back at Chase, who drifted far behind us now. He'd set their pace intentionally slow, despite Afonso trying to paddle faster. At least Chase understood what needed to happen.

I tried to imagine what this experience would be like alone, without my boss judging my every move and a whiny bride sharing my kayak. If I were alone, I would paddle all around the island, just for fun. I would drink in the sound of seagulls overhead and let the sunshine beat through the wind that kept tossing my hair into my eyes. I'd let the waves take me wherever they wanted and really explore this beautiful island. Yes, I could definitely get used to this.

But first, I had to keep my job and all that came with it— including Kamia Holland.

I felt Chase's gaze on my back the entire way.

FIVE

Turned out Kamia's description wasn't far off. The black sand felt more like tiny pieces of scratching gravel that got stuck in my sandals. I picked my way carefully across the rocky blanket and toward the softness of the grassy line of trees, listening for Kamia's shrill voice on a wind that had started picking up. I only heard a word here and there.

Chase stood back, watching Kamia and Afonso as they stood on the shore and talked in low voices. He wore a deep frown.

I understood why. If Kamia was this blatant with her unexpected crush, we could have a serious problem on our hands. Marcus would be sure to hear about this. If she canceled the wedding, what would happen to my job? I honestly didn't know. Maybe Chase's company only got a percentage of its money in the case of cancellations. For a wedding that cost six million dollars, that could be a significant sum. Her guests were already arriving.

Then again, Kamia was an adult, nearly thirty, and

certainly old enough to make her own decisions. She'd hired us to give her a beautiful wedding, not run her life.

I stepped next to Chase. "You need to stop frowning. You'll scare the clients away. They're supposed to be having fun, remember?"

He scowled at Kamia. "She's supposed to be getting married. There's a difference."

"If there's a difference, you aren't doing it right."

I chuckled at the joke. He only blinked.

Tough crowd. "My point is, maybe it would be good to avoid glaring at the client for the next hour. There's this thing called 'making conversation' that we could try. Let me show you how it works. What got you into the event planning business?"

He only shoved his hands into his pockets and glared harder. "That would be my uncle."

"Oh? He offered you a job?"

He barked a laugh. "Not exactly. Let's just say he's the one who made me the delightful business owner I am today."

A world of layers hid beneath those words, and plenty of emotions too. I could tell by the tone of his voice. I snuck another peek and saw the hard set of his jaw, the flash of anger in his eyes. Whoa. The guy felt strongly about his uncle.

"I'm guessing he wasn't the take-you-out-for-ice-cream-on-your-birthday type."

"Not exactly."

Kamia threw back her head and laughed at something Afonso had said, touching his arm as she did.

"That's it," Chase growled and strode over. By the time he reached the couple, his smoldering anger had been reined in by a professional smile. "So Afonso. How long are you in town?"

"My tour group leaves tomorrow afternoon," the man said

in accented English. He kept his eyes on the bride even as he answered the question.

"A shame," Chase said, a false note of happiness in his voice. "I had hoped you could attend the rehearsal dinner tomorrow night. I'm sure Kamia could use more supportive faces there, being so far from home." He turned to Kamia. "What do you think?"

Her expression soured as Afonso stared at Chase, comprehension sinking in slowly. Then he turned back to Kamia. "You are getting married?"

She wasn't wearing her ring, I saw now. Not that I would have worn a rock that large on the ocean, but I doubted she'd thought of that. Maybe the poor guy had been her idea of a last fling before the wedding.

"In a matter of speaking," Kamia said, looking cornered. "But I'm not married yet."

I felt almost bad for her. A moment before, she'd been all lit up. Happy. I hadn't seen her wear a smile since her arrival on the island. What bride didn't smile when she saw her groom? Why would a woman about to get married hide in her hotel room while her husband-to-be explored the island, only to emerge in the company of the wedding planner without her ring?

Chase didn't get it. This was a person's life, not just a fancy event and millions of dollars. Her future. She had to be sure of this.

Not that it was my place to tell him...unless I wanted to lose my job and get sent off the island before Ty even arrived.

I swiped back to the files on my phone and found the document from earlier. Ty was scheduled to arrive on the island next week, where he and his fiancée would prepare for the wedding a week later.

As for the details of their stay, I had everything—flight info, their suite number, the itinerary for each day, orders for roses to be sent to their rooms along with flower-shaped chocolates and wine. Even a couples massage in their room.

My mood soured at that. We'd done a couples massage once. I'd been the one to introduce it to him, as a matter of fact. He'd never had a massage before me.

Afonso seemed to have recovered from his shock well, because Kamia already had him laughing again. Clearly he wasn't as put off about the wedding thing as Chase had expected. I could almost see the wheels turning in Chase's mind as he excused himself, probably trying to figure out the next plan of action to separate the two.

He stepped a dozen yards away and plunged his hands into his pockets again, looking out over the horizon with a wistful look on his face. His hair lifted, exposing his entire face in a way I'd never seen before. His jawline looked even more pronounced than usual, and his expression was one of worry.

Worry that he would lose a big account? Or worry that he would lose something far bigger?

I remembered his reference to an uncle and opened a new browser window on my phone. I had it in minutes—his uncle, Ralph McNetta, was a billionaire broker in Chicago. The guy had served time in Seattle for some shady dealings. He'd inherited his nephew upon his sister's death, but clearly didn't have time for or even want children. It seemed Chase had essentially raised himself.

As if feeling my gaze, he turned against the wind to look back at me. Our eyes locked.

Electricity shot across the entire beach like a lightning bolt, capturing my attention and refusing to allow me to look away. The intensity there, hiding behind his gaze, held me positively captive.

Remember Ty. The man I planned to marry. The man fate intended for me.

With the might of Hercules, I tore my gaze away and glanced toward the forest instead. As strange as the black sandy beach seemed, I did love the lush greenery of the canopy behind us. It truly did feel like a paradise.

"...not tidy at all," Kamia was saying, bringing my attention back to them. "I assumed it would be more like Hawaii, where everything has a place. I like things thought out, you know?"

Like affairs, I wanted to say.

Afonso looked thoughtful. "I prefer this way. Those Americanized parts of Hawaii feel too fake. I do not think beauty can be crafted. I think it must be natural, and this is as natural as you can find." He gave her a winning smile. "Just like you are naturally beautiful."

Eyes wide, the bride-to-be stared at the man. "Marcus has never once called me naturally beautiful. He likes everything perfect."

"Then he is a fool, because you are perfection as you are."

With each word, I could feel Ty slipping away. My turn to try. "Looks like everyone's preparing to leave, Kamia. Are you ready to head back now?"

"I suppose." She gave Afonso a shy smile. "I'm a little tired though. Would you mind being my kayak partner on the way back? Give my arms a break?"

"I would be pleased to accompany you. Shall we?" He held out his arm, which she took, and they headed for the kayaks tied to the dock.

Chase appeared at my side. By the worry in his expression, he'd heard their conversation too. "This wedding has to happen."

"I know."

"The welfare of the company depends on it."

That I didn't know. "Does it?"

He ignored my question, instead staring after the couple. "Yes," he said softly.

Uh oh. That didn't sound good. "Is the company in trouble?"

He clenched his sharp jaw. "This summer is our last chance. The two biggest weddings make up forty percent of our revenue this year—Kamia's and Veronica Loyal's wedding next week, to whatever poor sot she talked into marrying her."

Triple crap. The entire company's survival depended on a bride who clearly didn't love her fiancé and my ex-boyfriend's wedding? If I meant to break up one, I had to make sure the other went through. I couldn't tank Chase's company and then walk away.

"You aren't a Veronica Loyal fan then?" I asked carefully.

"Let's just say we know each other well. Well enough that I'm surprised she still chose my company to plan her wedding." He seemed to shake himself back to reality and snapped into character once again, his earlier vulnerability fading. "I guess we're kayak partners now. Better get going. I don't want to leave those two alone on the ocean."

Then something strange happened. His arm lifted, his elbow extended, as if he was offering it to me just as Afonso had offered his to Kamia. And he waited.

I imagined striding toward the kayaks with my arm looped in his and felt an odd plummeting sensation in my stomach. I knew that touching Chase would only make that sensation worse, and I couldn't say why. So I did the only thing I could think of.

I pretended not to see and headed for the kayak.

A moment later, I heard him follow. He said nothing, which I appreciated.

I felt guilty for rejecting his polite gesture, but I'd read about more than his childhood in that article. There were photos of women, dates he only took out a few times before dumping them. Relationships that only lasted a few weeks. Stories of rejection and pain whenever people tried to get too close. I'd already had my heart broken once in the past year.

I didn't need a guy like Chase to finish the job.

SIX

SEVEN YEARS EARLIER

I swung my duffel bag over my shoulder and strode toward the back door of my family's farmhouse. As a nineteen-year-old freshman at the local community college, I'd spent most of the past year studying or sitting in class. With my last final submitted and summer officially here, I could celebrate with Bridget.

Freedom. It felt so good.

I had my hand on the doorknob when I heard a pained grunt coming from the direction of the hallway. Stopping to listen only yielded a few whispers.

Odd. My parents didn't need to whisper. I was the only child, and we were alone in the house.

I tiptoed toward my parents' bedroom and found Mom standing in the doorway, pulling the door closed. I caught sight of Dad on the bed, grimacing.

"Another bad day?" I asked. He'd been recovering from an infection for a few weeks now. Mom, ever the protector, hadn't allowed me in to see him so I wouldn't introduce new germs. She kept insisting he would be fine with rest, but I'd been concerned about the paleness of his face under the baseball cap he wore almost constantly.

"Oh, it isn't that," Mom said. Her eyes were pinched at the corners, and her usual smile was missing. "He had a little procedure done today. I just gave him some painkillers, so he should be fine soon."

My breath hitched. "Procedure? Was it his lungs?"

"No, no, nothing like that. Just a root canal. A tooth that's been bothering him for weeks."

That made sense, but my mom seemed unusually edgy today. Even now, she shifted her weight from one foot to another and glanced around the hallway, as if she couldn't wait to end this conversation.

"I was going to Bridget's to sleep over," I told her, "but I'll stay to help here instead."

Mom waved a hand. "Don't be silly. I have this handled, so go have fun with your friend."

Her earlier nervousness had fled, replaced by my no-nonsense mother. While I felt better about the situation, I didn't want to leave her alone to care for Dad either. "Is there anything you need from town? I can go to the pharmacy and be back in thirty minutes."

Her tone was flat. "Daphne, go. I'll see you tomorrow."

"Fine. Okay." I gave her a quick hug and headed for the stables to the west where my mare, Rosie, grazed. Her behavior made more sense than my own parents' did these days. As an adopted child, they'd never made me feel like I didn't belong. But not being able to enter my own father's room to bring him comfort after a root canal?

Sometimes Mom took the whole 'control freak' thing to a new level.

Rosie nickered when she saw me and started over. I would ride her through town and let her graze with Bridget's Appaloosa gelding, Westley, in their field. The two horses got along almost as well as their owners.

When we arrived at Bridget's, she already had everything ready—a Magic 8 ball, the newspaper with today's horoscopes, and even a bowl of fortune cookies. A book entitled "The Palm Reader's Guide to Everything" sat open on her mattress. The only thing missing was a ouija board, but I had to draw the line somewhere.

"Ready to plan your future?" she asked.

I sat on her bed. "I only wanted to figure out my major."

"Well, you won't have to do it alone. We have the power of the universe at our disposal." She gave her hands a wave, revealing thick bracelets full of colorful stones.

I laughed. My parents thought I was the eccentric one, but recently, Bridget had taken our astrology teenage obsession to a whole new level. "Okay, but if the universe tells me to major in Accounting, I'll have some words to say. Not nice words."

"Some math is important. Like counting your boyfriends."

I elbowed her in the ribs. "You're the only one who needs calculus to figure that out."

"Nope. I'm staying right here in my comfy small town and kissing respectable farmers. You're the one going to New York when you get your bachelor's and becoming a millionaire CEO with fabulous designer clothes and a line of hot, rich boyfriends. I guarantee that someday, you'll kiss two hot guys in a single day, and you better tell me when it happens. Better yet, I want a gallon of ice cream delivered to my door. Rocky Road. With a huge container of chocolate sauce. Better yet, chocolate sauce *on* my chocolate sauce."

I covered my heart and raised my hand to the sky. "If that actually happens, and it won't, may I lose both boyfriends and come eat ice cream with you." I paused. "Actually, ice cream sounds really good. Should we go?"

"You work there. Aren't you tired of Bennie's yet?"

"Never."

She grinned. "Deal. But you're paying. Employee discount for the win."

Ten minutes later, we arrived at the ice cream shop and waited in line. It seemed surprisingly long today, and we had to stand outside. By the time we reached the counter, Bridget and I were both sweating and very ready for Bennie's famous chocolate sundaes.

But when I flashed Bennie a smile behind the register, he frowned.

My stomach sank a little. Was I supposed to be working today? I almost grabbed my phone to check the schedule before remembering I had all week off, something that rarely happened.

"Two Bennie's giant sundaes. You know the way we like them." I looked around at the overflowing tables. "Do you need me today after all?"

He blinked and his frown deepened. Was that disapproval? "Figured you'd be at home with your dad. Yet you're out getting ice cream with friends."

My dad. Taking care of him from that dental surgery? What a strange thing for my boss to say. "Nah, he's fine. Just sleeping it off."

His eyes bugged, but he said nothing more as he turned and prepared our sundaes. When he reached us, his mouth pressed in a hard, firm line. "You go be with him after this, you hear?" He turned away, muttering something that sounded like "If I had a daughter like that..."

Bridget and I looked at each other, completely baffled, and found a table. No less than three adults turned to look my direction, their expressions immediately disapproving.

What in the world?

I felt numb. Something deep inside whispered that I was missing something, that Bennie knew something I didn't but really should.

I didn't eat much of my sundae. Bridget talked nearly the entire time, but I barely heard her. Finally, I told her I was going to the restroom but rounded toward the kitchen instead, where Bennie was tying off a garbage bag.

"What did you mean by that?" I asked quietly. "That I should be with my dad."

He guffawed and turned away. "I'm beginning to wonder about you, kid. You work hard, but is this really the time to be eating ice cream with friends? If there were ever a time your dad needed you, it's now."

I thought about that glimpse of Dad this morning, groaning in pain. Mom closing the door quickly so I wouldn't see.

Her fumbling words that had to be lies. The guilt in her eyes.

I was such an idiot.

"Tell me what you've heard," I demanded.

Bennie stared at me with a dark expression. He must have seen the truth in my eyes, because he sighed. "If your parents haven't told you, that's something you need to hear from them."

A very diplomatic answer.

I'd have to put the clues together myself. Mom's excuses,

refusing to let me into their room because of germs, Dad's hat. More pale every day. Some kind of surgery . . .

"I've got to go," I told him, hurrying toward the door.

"Yeah, you gotta. Don't come back to work till everything's sorted, you hear? I can give you another week if you need."

SEVEN

WALKING home from the kayaking tour, I picked my way along the path and admired the jungle-like plants around me. Birds I'd never seen before sang in the trees, and the sky overhead remained a gray-blue as the clouds cleared and prepared for night to descend on the scene.

This island was positively stunning. Now I just had to figure out how to get Kamia to go through with her wedding so I wouldn't have to leave it within days of my arrival. Maybe if I got the bride and groom together, they could work things out. A reservation at the hotel restaurant perhaps? Another gift basket? I couldn't think of a single thing other than physically following Kamia around to keep her away from her handsome new crush. She and Afonso had said goodbye shortly after the kayaking expedition, but it hadn't been a *goodbye forever* goodbye. It had been a *I'll see you soon* goodbye. Whatever Kamia had planned, it could not be good for Chase's bottom line.

Bride-sitting had definitely *not* been in my job description.

"Hey, wedding planner!"

I turned to find the pool guy from the other day hurrying

toward me, the one who'd argued with Chase. He pulled up and grinned. The guy wore a hat to cover his balding head today, and his khaki collared shirt lay open to reveal a hairy, deeply tanned chest.

I returned his smile. "Hello again."

"I heard you had to share a kayak with the big guy. How did that go?" There was an amused twinkle in his dark eyes.

I snorted. "About as well as you can imagine."

"Hey, if you managed not to get fired for wearing the wrong color shirt, you're ahead of most of us."

I gave him a long look. The Chase I'd seen, the one who argued with this man, had been the same gruff boss who'd sent me to this island. But the Chase I'd just spent three hours with seemed different, like he carried the weight of the world on his shoulders. "He does seem worried about the business, but I would be too."

"*Querida muchacha,*" he said, putting a hand on his chest as if I'd hurt him. "I assure you, he's far worse than you think. Once you're on Chase Everett's radar, you're only one billionaire-tantrum away from utter poverty."

Four days before, I'd been in near poverty, but Chase's offer had pulled me out of it. Thanks to his signing bonus, I'd been able to pay one of my two months' late rent. The next paycheck would take care of the rest. In fact, if I weren't planning to steal a groom, this promotion could have lifted me to a far better apartment by this time next year.

If only.

But that didn't mean the pool guy had had the same experience with Chase. "Did he fire someone you know?" I asked.

The man scowled. "He hired six of us a few months ago before . . . what is the word, downsizing? I'm the only one left, but not because he likes me. Hard to work when he's hovering and glaring at you every two seconds, you know?"

That, I did know. "Sure."

"Well, anyway, some of the staff are meeting at the outdoor bar for drinks tonight at 10:30. You should come."

I intended to be long asleep by then. Even now, I felt another lack-of-sleep headache coming on. "I'll have to skip tonight, but next time."

"If you say so. Another time, wedding planner. Assuming you're still around." He chuckled and trotted away.

💙💙💙💙💙

The next morning, I felt far more refreshed. I arrived to work at 7:58 a.m., looking around in case Chase was stalking me again. But the man was nowhere to be seen.

A new stack of work sat on my desk, problems waiting to be solved. I could only hope none of them involved brides having second thoughts.

I thumbed through the stack. An accident in the storage room that broke several tables and made us short a few. We'd have to rent some in town. The chicken problem was solved, but the kitchen's manager was out sick and would likely be gone for tonight's rehearsal dinner. The aide would be on the job, they assured me, and everything would go according to plan.

I felt sick. What else could possibly go wrong with this blasted wedding?

The phone in my pocket buzzed. An unfamiliar number had sent a text.

My thumb hovered over the screen for a moment as I decided whether I had the bandwidth for this right now.

Shouldn't I handle one problem at a time? But this could be pressing. I opened the screen and scanned the text.

This is Marcus Latimer. Have you seen Kamia? She disappeared last night after dinner.

I muttered a curse. The woman's rehearsal dinner was just eight hours from now, and I'd prepared the freaking chicken myself. What more did she want me to do? How could I answer this question without making everything blow up in our faces? It wasn't like I could tell the groom *Sorry, but she's having an affair with a hot, young tourist from Portugal. I'm sure she'll be back before the wedding.*

Instead, I went through six different versions before finally responding as vaguely as possible.

Hi Marcus! I haven't seen her, but I'll try to track her down and get back to you soon.

Then I picked up the radio. "Agwe, are you there?"

He answered immediately. "Hi Daphne, I am here."

"We have a missing bride. Kamia Holland. Can you help me gather a few people to search for her?"

There was a pause that lasted almost a full minute. Then he finally responded. "Found her. The grounds crew say she is on the north side, Cabana 4. Would you like me to go?"

"No, I'll do it. Thank you." I hooked the radio back to my belt with a sigh.

I was *so* not getting paid enough for this. A wedding planner put a wedding together. She wasn't supposed to act as the couple's therapist. If there was one thing I *didn't* know how to do, it was healing broken relationships.

The past seven years were proof enough of that.

EIGHT

WHEN I ARRIVED at the cabana, I saw a pair of perfectly pedicured feet sticking out one end. Only one. At least she was alone.

I peered around the canvas and stifled a groan. Nope, not alone. Her Portuguese friend sat next to her lounge chair, sipping a drink with a little umbrella in it and reading. Kamia lay in a gold bikini with sequins, wearing thick sunglasses.

Afonso spotted me and rested his book on his knee. "She's asleep."

"May I?" I asked.

He gestured to the other end of the lounge chair. I took a seat, unsure how to broach the subject. I needed to discuss this with Kamia, not her Portuguese love muffin.

"Her fiancé is looking for her," I finally said.

He blew out a long breath. "I know. He's been texting her since last night, but she refuses to answer. She drank too much and passed out. I didn't want to leave her here alone."

I looked around the cabana. At least they hadn't spent the

night in his room. Assuming he was telling the truth. "So you stayed with her here all night?"

"I asked a worker to watch her while I grabbed my book. It took maybe ten minutes. Other than that, yes." He shot her an uncertain look. "I don't know what's going on. She doesn't want to leave him, but she doesn't seem to love him either."

Silence fell between us. Kamia's chest rose and fell in sleep, gentle and slow. Her mouth hung slightly open. She looked human. Vulnerable. Like a woman who only wanted to be happy. If I hadn't known her, I would never have guessed this woman would be a multi-millionaire by tomorrow evening.

"She's obviously attracted to you," I said.

He nodded. "She is a very attractive woman. I would like to get to know her better. But I live across the ocean, and I don't want to break up a relationship if it could bring her joy."

I don't want to break up a relationship if it could bring her joy.

I immediately thought of Ty's relationship. Did it bring him joy? Would his fiancée cheat on him?

Or would he cheat on her...with me?

A flood of guilt and remorse overcame me then, which I immediately pushed back. Ty had been interested that day in the office. I knew it. That meant their relationship couldn't be right, and I would be the one to save him. I refused to stand back and watch him make the biggest mistake of his life.

"She's the only one who can make that choice, I'm afraid," I told him. "The sooner, the better. Preparations for her rehearsal dinner are underway. Most of the wedding party is already here. They'll be suspicious about her disappearance soon if they aren't already, and I'm sure the groom is out of his mind with worry."

"I'm sure he's not," Kamia muttered, rolling over. She

wiped a wayward piece of hair from her face and groaned. "You both talk so loud."

Afonso's hand tightened on his book. "We need to talk. Where do you see this going?"

"Going?" She yawned. "I don't know. Can't I just stay here for a few more hours? But with the flaps closed. It's too bright."

"A few more hours?" Afonso's jaw clenched. "You want me to entertain you until your wedding dinner, and then turn you over to your fiancé like the past day never happened?"

"No? Sort of." She put her head in her hands. "I don't know."

He stood and tossed his book aside. "I'm not looking for a fling. When I give myself to a woman, it will be forever. I will expect the same in return. That seems like something you can't give. Not to him, not to me."

"Afonso—"

"I'm going to the airport. My flight home leaves at 1:30 p.m. I hope you can make your decision by then." He swiped his book off the sand, stalked out of the cabana, and disappeared.

Kamia watched him go and straightened her sunglasses. "Why are men always so jealous?"

I had a hundred answers to that, none of which were very nice. So I kept my frustration inside and fell back on my professional role. "Look, I'm just the wedding planner. All I need to know is whether there will still be a wedding tomorrow."

Kamia took her sunglasses off and fixed her gaze on me. "So do I."

I shuddered inwardly at her appearance. She'd obviously been crying, because her eyes were puffy and bloodshot. The remnants of yesterday's mascara pooled under her eyes, dried and flaking.

"Marcus is looking for you," I said. "I promised to notify him the second I found you."

"But you won't, will you." It wasn't a question.

I swept all thoughts of Chase and his impossible expectations out of my mind. "If you ask me not to, I won't."

She looked surprised. "The other planner definitely would have ratted me out. Like, way before now."

I took Afonso's place on the lounge chair across from her. "I'm not the other wedding planner. I do want to know what's going on though. Did you have a fight?"

She watched me for a long moment before leaning closer, lowering her voice. "Marcus...isn't a nice man."

I'd met the guy, and I could have told her that at first glance. I only nodded and chose my words carefully. "He does seem a little brusque."

She pulled her knees to her chest and stared at the sandy floor. "He hurts me sometimes," she said softly.

A sinking feeling sat in the pit of my stomach. No wonder she was having second thoughts. "No one deserves to be treated like that. Especially by someone who claims to love you."

She sniffed. "Except he's never said he loves me. Not once."

I swallowed. Ty wasn't perfect, but at least he'd been able to say those three important words. "I'm sorry."

"Marcus says I'm beautiful," she continued, her tone bitter, "but there's always a 'but.' Like he wishes I would tone my stomach a little more. Or he likes the sound of my voice, but I use it too much. Or I have good taste in clothes, but I spend too much of his money. But, but, but. Never enough. Always lacking. He'll brag to people that I have a Master's degree and then joke that it was obviously a waste of time and money. Right there, with everyone laughing in my face." Her eyes flicked to the chair Afonso had just vacated. "He would never have sat by my side all night until I felt better."

Silence fell upon the cabana, broken only by the distant

sound of waves, shrieking seagulls, and the quiet pain of a young woman's heart.

I knew what Chase expected of me. He wanted this wedding to go through at any cost.

But that was the difference between me and him—I couldn't be okay with that. Not when it meant a lifetime of abuse and misery for another human being. Nothing was worth that. Not all the money in the entire world.

"I thought I could endure it till he died, and I could live as a widow in peace," Kamia continued. "But I don't think I can take another week with that man, let alone take his name forever. Since we've been together, I've completely lost myself. I didn't realize it until I stepped into that kayak yesterday. Afonso treats me like a completely different person. I like who I am with him."

I like who I am with him.

Had I liked who I was with Ty? We'd been completely wrapped up in each other at first. But our relationship had felt strained over time when he won every argument, chose every restaurant, and dominated or ended every conversation. With each day that passed, I felt more and more like Cinderella's stepsister—the one trying to fit her too-large foot into a tiny glass slipper.

But Veronica Loyal, of all people? He'd fallen for the first heiress to come along, and the entire world had to see that they didn't belong together. If I didn't save him, nobody would.

Kamia, on the other hand, had nobody else to save her. Marriage and family relationships were hard enough without abuse. If a bad marriage could be avoided, didn't I have a commission from humanity to try, Chase Everett or not? Surely rich people deserved happiness too.

If only this didn't feel as if I had to choose between helping Kamia and winning Ty back.

With an internal sigh, I leaned forward as Kamia dabbed at her eyes. "There's a quote I love from a cowboy movie. It says, 'If you're going to sprint, make sure it's because you're chasing your future and not running from your past.' It sounds like you already know what you want. You're just afraid to chase it."

Kamia's eyes ducked. "Because it's terrifying."

I took her manicured hand and gave her a level stare. "Maybe so. But at least you won't need to be afraid anymore. Think what that will be like."

I watched as Kamia's shoulders rounded, her back straightened, and her expression changed. "You're right." She sniffed and straightened. "No, really. You're right. I know exactly what I need to do. I need to disappear. Far away, somewhere Marcus will never find me."

Somewhere like Portugal. She didn't have to say it aloud. I saw the decision in her eyes, her posture, and her hopeful expression.

"I don't have to do this." Her voice was full of realization, of wonder. "Thank you, wedding planner. What's your name again?"

"Daphne Porter," I said, marveling at this instant change in her. The fear was completely gone.

"There's one more thing you can do for me, Daphne Porter. Continue preparations for tonight's dinner, but I'll text Marcus to meet me at the waterfall near the front of the resort in one hour. I want you and Chase there too."

Oh, boy. This would be fun to explain to Chase. "You've got it." I stood and started away.

"Daphne?"

I turned back. "Yes?"

Kamia stared at me, looking all lit up inside. She looked like a completely different person from the shriveled woman I'd found sleeping in this cabana a few minutes before. "Thanks a lot."

"I'm here to serve."

NINE

I was most definitely *NOT* here to serve.

As I approached the waterfall, I found Chase standing there with his arms folded. He didn't look happy.

"They aren't here yet?" I asked, looking around at the tropical flowers and the gorgeous water feature. The water fell gently, creating an audible backdrop of sound that felt immediately relaxing. It would have been a beautiful site for a wedding proposal or even a reception. But I had a feeling it would serve as quite the opposite today.

"Not yet," Chase said. "Before they arrive, I need to know what's going on."

I hadn't told him in the text. How could I possibly explain in a way that wouldn't get me fired in two seconds? This way, at least he could see it for himself.

"I'm not entirely sure," I said carefully. "The bride asked the groom to meet her here and wanted us both to come along. Maybe she wanted witnesses."

"Or emotional support," he muttered. "She's calling it off. This can't be happening."

"We get paid either way, right?" I said. "I mean, we've done our job. All the details have been taken care of. Surely the contract covers us in cases like this."

He ran a hand through his hair in frustration. "It does," he said, "usually. But in this case, the groom must have had an inkling that his bride would run, because he insisted on adding a clause that he would only pay the full amount if everything went smoothly. If not, we would only receive a quarter of the fee. I authorized the change myself, thinking it worth the risk for such a lucrative account."

Wow. He must have really believed this wedding would go through. That, or he'd been almost desperate to win this contract. I remembered his lecture back in New York about everything being perfect. It wasn't the perfectionist in him or even the stern boss—it was the fact that our business literally depended on it. My decision to help Kamia had even greater implications than I'd assumed.

"Hello, everyone," Kamia called from the path. She'd showered and styled her hair in loose, wind-blown waves. She wore an ankle-length sundress that rustled in the soft breeze and looked more relaxed than I'd ever seen her. "Thank you both for coming."

Chase grumbled something under his breath. I doubted it was a polite greeting.

I checked my watch. "It's five past. Marcus should arrive any second."

"He won't be here for another minute or two. Marcus doesn't like me ordering him around, so he tries to show me who's in charge. Yet another reason for this meeting."

Chase put on his professional smile and cleared his throat. "Look, Kamia, I'm sorry to hear that your relationship has been strained since your arrival—"

"Since forever," Kamia corrected. "I didn't ask you here for your opinion, Mr. Everett. I only wanted you to see."

"See what?"

"Kamia!" Marcus roared from the pathway, his voice carrying easily over the sound of the waterfall. The moment he saw us, he slowed, looking confused.

She turned and flashed him a brilliant smile. "Good to see you too, love. I'm glad to see you missed me."

"My fiancée disappears all night and then I find out she's with some foreign tourist," he snapped, finally reaching her.

Kamia met his gaze firmly. There was a strain in her expression, though, that said this was harder for her than it looked. "You're imagining the worst, but it wasn't like that. I got drunk and spent the night sprawled across a lounge chair in a cabana."

"Do you think I'm a fool?" he practically spat at her. "You two were inseparable yesterday. I have multiple reports of you throwing yourself at him. Photos, even. Then you're gone all night, and I'm supposed to believe you just fell asleep and it's all innocent?"

"Yes. You're supposed to believe what I say when it's the truth."

His hand twitched, and I knew he was thinking about hitting her. Now I understood why she wanted us here—not as moral support or even witnesses, but as bodyguards. He wouldn't dare hurt her as long as we were watching.

"Let's go inside and talk about this," he said, lowering his voice.

"You're here to listen, not talk," she said evenly. "Here's what's going to happen. I won't be marrying you. In fact, I'm climbing on an airplane in about two hours, and I hope to never see you again. You, however, will attend our rehearsal dinner and assure our friends that we split amicably. You'll ensure that they have a good time here and leave happy."

Marcus looked positively purple. "You will not humiliate me in front of several dozen of the most powerful people in the world. You'll go through with it if I have to drag you down the aisle."

"The wedding oaths are voluntary," I pointed out. "Do you really want her to say no in front of all those people? That would be far more embarrassing. She's doing you a favor."

His head snapped around, and he crossed over to me, his forefinger stabbing me in the collarbone. "How dare you insert yourself into this conversation, wedding planner. If you'd done your job and kept her from Hunka-Hunka-Latin Boy, none of this would have happened."

Then Chase was there, standing between us. "Touch Daphne again, and you'll regret it." His voice was low and dangerous.

Marcus tried to sidestep him, still giving me a murderous look, but Chase remained solidly in his way.

"Your wedding planner was with her, Everett," Marcus snapped. "She knew what was going on and didn't say a word about it! I have witnesses. What kind of wedding planner enables an affair right out in the open? You'll send her packing if you know what's good for you." The man looked like he would spit in my face if Chase weren't there.

"Your relationship problems are not Daphne's fault," Chase said, his voice containing an edge of barely controlled anger. "Stand down now."

"Stand down?" Marcus huffed. "Some help you are. My fiancée doesn't know what she's saying. Keep the arrangements as planned." Marcus spun and stormed over to Kamia, who yelped as he grabbed her wrist and began to drag her toward the hotel.

I hurried to block their escape, but to my surprise, Chase was already there.

"Kamia is no longer your fiancée," Chase said. "Remove your hand, or I'll have you arrested for assault."

"She's hung over, Everett. Spouting nonsense. Go do your job and get the wedding stuff ready so you can get paid. I'll handle her." His hand tightened on Kamia's arm, making her gasp in pain.

In a split second, Chase had Marcus doubled over, his arm twisted in a hold behind his back that had the older man sputtering. Marcus finally released Kamia and flailed his free arm about, trying to free himself.

"Daphne," Chase said calmly, not budging an inch. "Accompany Kamia to her room to gather her belongings. I'll have a car waiting out front to take her to the airport. In the meantime, Marcus and I will have a little chat with security."

"You aren't getting a cent from me, Everett," Marcus managed, wriggling in Chase's grip like a helpless worm. "How dare you touch me? I'll sue you for everything you have."

I pulled Kamia toward the hotel, and we trotted away at a run, leaving the men to face each other down. When we reached her room and locked the door behind us, Kamia's expression looked utterly transformed—joy and relief. No more fear.

"Did that just happen?" she asked breathlessly. "I know I was there, but . . . I can't believe Chase did that."

"Neither can I," I said, still a bit in shock. I'd expected him to fire me for this, not join me in her emancipation.

But the thing that startled me the most about everything was Chase's reaction to Marcus confronting me. Instant protectiveness. No, more than that. He'd looked positively enraged, like he'd wanted to pummel my accuser rather than simply subdue him.

I wasn't sure how to feel about that.

Kamia packed faster than I thought possible, and then a

waiting security team escorted us to the lobby and a waiting car. As the driver took her bags and loaded them into the back, I spotted more bodyguards filling the remainder of the seats. Kamia would be better protected than the president today.

Kamia threw herself at me, squeezing tight. "Thank you," she whispered into my ear.

Then she was gone.

TEN

SEVEN YEARS EARLIER

THE MOMENT I walked in through the garage door, my suspicions were confirmed. No less than four casseroles sat on the countertop, all covered with tin foil and waiting to be put into a fridge that hadn't been cleaned out in weeks. The low murmur of conversation hummed from the living room. Several visitors, all women from what I could hear. My mom's voice was among them.

I skipped the living room and took the back hallway to my parents' bedroom. Opening the door slowly so the hinges wouldn't creak, I tiptoed quietly to the bed, blinking to let my eyes adjust to the darkness. The room smelled stale with the sharp twang of antiseptic—very different from the vanilla-lavender spray Mom constantly used. I hated it immediately.

Dad lay awake, staring at nothing. When I reached him, his eyes focused on me.

I folded my arms, feeling more uncomfortable than I ever had in my life, but knowing I had to get this out. "It's cancer, isn't it?"

Dad tried to talk and coughed instead. I stood there awkwardly, ready to pound on his back if it came to that, but he finally sat back with a deep sigh.

"Who told you?" he managed.

My hands curled into fists. Rather than answering the question, he wanted to know how I knew? "Nobody." My voice shook. With anger or fear, I couldn't tell. "But a girl suspects things when she walks through town and people think she's a terrible daughter for being there and not here, not to mention the casseroles and well-wishers in the living room. It feels like a funeral in here."

"I'm not dying. This thing won't lick me yet."

I pounded the bed with one fist. "How dare you keep this from me?" My voice wobbled again, but I didn't care. "You and Mom both. I feel like a stranger in my own home!"

His gaze turned back to me, and I saw a glint of anger there. "I wouldn't let her tell you. My decision, Daphne. I'll lick this thing and send it right back to where it came from. Soon everyone will forget it ever happened."

"Forget? You've got to be kidding me."

"No use in everyone getting worked up."

"Worked up?" My voice sounded shrill, loud. Not me at all. "So you let Mom tell everyone else in town but not me? Do you have any idea how that feels?"

"We planned to tell you, just not right away."

"A secret." I put my hands on my hips. "You really thought you could keep this a secret from your own daughter, and everything would be okay."

"It. Is. Okay. They got the cancer out. I'll be walking

around by tomorrow and working the fields again by Monday. This isn't anything you need to concern yourself about."

"But the people in town can worry instead? What am I, the family dog that you feed and send on her way to chase birds in the fields?"

Dad took two shallow breaths before responding, his voice strained. "Of course not. We just want you to lead a normal life."

I snorted. "Is it normal for your boss at the ice cream shop to know more about your own father than you? The mayor's wife, whose truck is parked out front? I even heard the mailman's girlfriend in the living room. It's good to know where I stand."

"Daphne Porter, stop jumping to conclusions. We waited to tell you for your own good. Some secrets are meant to protect."

Protect? I felt wetness on my cheek and wiped it angrily with my shirt sleeve. Here I stood, almost twenty years old, still living in my parents' house and being treated like the four-year-old I'd been when they took me in. Clearly that was how they would always see me.

"Keeping me in the dark is not protecting," I growled, taking satisfaction in the fact that his eyes dropped to the blanket. "And some secrets do nothing but hurt."

ELEVEN

WITH THE NEXT day's schedule cleared with the departure of the bride, I found myself taking a walk into town, my favorite bag slung over my shoulder. The sky seemed a bright silver color today, the sun peering through the occasional crack in the clouds as if seeking an opening to break through. Lucious greenery surrounded me on all sides, a constant reminder that I was far from New York. Paradise indeed.

Upon returning to the waterfall area yesterday, I'd discovered that Chase had physically subdued Marcus until security could arrive, the man spewing all the while that he would sue. After the man threw a few punches, security had cuffed and dumped him off at the police station. The rehearsal dinner had gone on as planned despite the missing bride and groom, although that was likely because Chase had announced to the crowd that the couple had split amicably and wished everyone a wonderful vacation regardless. He'd even upgraded their alcohol package to keep everyone happy, something that wouldn't have made me blink an eye except I knew what it would cost him.

We wouldn't be getting paid. Not for the dinner, the wedding, the hotel rooms, nothing. Not without an expensive legal battle that would only cost Chase more money.

So why had he helped me with Kamia?

The question had haunted me all night. Walking wasn't quite enough to distract me from Chase and his weird behavior yesterday. With the tourists huddled in their rooms, Kamia gone, and Marcus still in custody for another few hours, there would be little to do today until preparations began for the next wedding.

Ty's wedding.

He'd be arriving tomorrow, and I still didn't have a real plan. Between kayaking and Chase and Kamia and everything that came with this job, I'd barely had time to do anything but crash each night. But what could I do, other than look for the right moment to talk to Ty?

Hey, I know we broke up, I imagined myself saying, *but I'm still in love with you, and I've decided you're still in love with me. Plus, a fortune cookie and my horoscope both say we're getting married, which pretty much means we're meant to be. So ditch your beautiful model heiress with her millions and join me in poverty in New York, okay?*

Yeah. Not likely to go well.

My phone buzzed. I whipped it from my pocket and frowned. My mom.

I lifted it to my ear, feeling that familiar jolt of worry. "Hey, Mom. Is Dad all right?"

"Hi, baby girl!" she exclaimed. "Of course he's all right. Just checking in on that amazing promotion. Are you getting super tan and loving it? Seeing lots of crocodiles? Meeting lots of boys?"

Meeting lots of boys? I gritted my teeth. Mom still thought of me as thirteen years old. "It's going great. As for the crocodiles...not really." Mom was obsessed with crocodiles. She loved them like shark people loved Shark Week, and I still had no idea why. There were no crocodiles in Arkansas. "And yes to the tan, but I'm too busy to date right now."

"Nonsense. It doesn't take any time at all to flirt with a guy here and there. I'm sure those islanders are hunky and sweet."

"Many of them are, but I'm not here to date." I was here to steal a husband instead. No big deal.

"That's when things happen, when you're least expecting it. At least stay open to the idea, all right? You never know when Cupid's arrow will strike. There's something special about tropical islands. Not that I've ever been to one, but that's what I've heard."

I thought about Kamia and smiled slightly, wondering if she'd gone home with Afonso after all.

"Do you remember Ty?" I asked, regretting the question the instant I'd voiced it.

"Yes. Why?" I didn't miss the false note of enthusiasm in her tone.

Because I'm going to sabotage his wedding. I'm stealing him away, and I won't let myself feel guilty because fate wants us together.

But I worry that I can't keep him.

That last part came from the dark recesses of my soul, and the strength of it surprised me. If I'd lost Ty once before, what would stop it from happening again? If I could tear him away from the woman he intended to marry so easily, didn't that mean someone else could tear him away from me?

"No reason," I finally said. "I ran into him the other day at the office is all."

"Aww. I'm sure that was hard."

Not in the least. "It's fine, Mom. I'm fine. You don't need to worry about me. I'm good at finding my own happiness."

There was a long pause.

"What?" I asked, confused about her hesitation.

"I want you to be happy," she said carefully. "I do. Pray for it every morning and night and plenty of times in-between. But it doesn't seem like you've found anything of the sort, because you keep looking inside other people and in these distant places. Anywhere but inside of you or with your family, where you'll actually find it. Baby girl, this island of yours may seem perfect on the outside, but it could be keeping you from making genuine connections. Just like New York did."

I wasn't ready for this conversation. "Mom. If you're trying to get me to return to Arkansas, it isn't happening."

"The people here are real. They care about one another. I may not live there, but New York people are snobbish and impatient. It seems like a lonely way of life."

"They only seem that way until you get to know them. Look, I have things to do. I have Ty—I mean, I have to get ready for next week's wedding. It'll be the biggest one of the summer, and my job depends on it." She was wrong. I would find happiness with Ty and we'd rebuild our life together in New York, far from the stresses of home. A few short days from now, everything would be fine.

"All right," Mom said, "but keep one thing in mind. If this job doesn't work out just like the others didn't, come home. Your room looks exactly like it did the day you left. We'll get you back on your feet in no time."

Yeah, I bet they would. Mom had no idea how close I was to crawling back home on my hands and knees. I had no car, no savings, and barely the clothes on my back, even here.

"Thanks, Mom," I told her. "You've always been there for me, and I appreciate it."

"You enjoy yourself, all right? Work is good for the heart, but free time is good for the soul."

"You got it."

When I hung up, I noticed the rain picking up again. I'd wandered a good couple miles from the resort without even knowing it. Wishing I'd thought to bring an umbrella, I found a bus stop sign and huddled beneath it as my hair got flatter and flatter, sending rain dripping down my face. A group of tourists carrying umbrellas crowded me more with each passing minute.

After what felt like forever, a bus finally pulled up. A sign in the window said CROCODILE TOUR: 3000 colones.

"No other bus," the driver called. "Only me."

Ha. Well, Mom was getting her crocodile photos sooner than either of us expected. Maybe this would distract her from her life lessons and guilt trips.

I dug a wad of money from my pocket and handed it to the driver. He dipped his head and motioned to the back. Before I'd even taken two steps, the bus started to move.

Plopping into an empty seat, I looked around. All Asian tourists who ignored my presence. Fine by me.

It took about twenty minutes to arrive at the crocodile place, wherever that was. I filed out with the others and came face-to-face with a nondescript bridge over muddy water.

"A bridge," I muttered to myself, following the others. This wasn't what I'd expected. A swamp, maybe, but a random bridge in the middle of the rainforest? I probably could have picked a better excursion for my day off. At least the drizzle had stopped.

The tour guide began to speak in Japanese. Lovely. Well, I didn't need to know trivia about crocodiles to take photos of them.

I walked closer to the river, stepping softly, and stared under the bridge. It looked like a pile of logs beneath the brown water at first. Then I gave a little gasp and whipped out my

phone, zooming in. Sure enough, those logs were actually crocodiles. Only my phone wouldn't zoom in quite close enough for
a good photo. A different angle, then. I rounded the bank and
drew closer.

At that moment, a gust of wind sent my shoulder bag flying
into the river.

Grumbling, I stepped closer, wincing at the muddy bank
that tried to claim my sandals. Then I reached over, holding to
a tree for balance and straining to grip the edge of my bag. I
managed to close two fingers around it, but the second I started
pulling, the water swirled it out of reach again by a few inches.

I looked down. My feet were already half-covered in mud.
One more step wouldn't make any difference.

"Come on," I growled at my hat, stepping into the murky
water. But it gave way beneath my feet. I scrambled for the tree,
but the ground under one foot continued to move, keeping me
unsteady. I stumbled and nearly fell right into the water—

A strong arm snaked around my waist and yanked me back
to shore.

I gasped, finding myself clutched against a firm chest. A
man exhaled next to my ear. *Musky outdoors.* I knew that scent.

"Daphne," Chase hissed. "What were you thinking?"

"I only wanted my bag," I grumbled, pulling free and
turning to look at him. Chase Everett wore a gray tee today and
denim shorts with a buckle belt. His hair looked wilder than
usual, and his chin sported an extra day's worth of stubble.

"Another second, and you would have lost your leg. Maybe
worse," he said, pointing at the river. It swirled slightly where
I'd just been standing, but strangely. Unnaturally.

Oh.

"Just because you can't see them, doesn't mean they aren't
there. Didn't you see the sign?"

Now I did—a great wooden contraption at the trail

entrance with a crocodile's face on it. I couldn't even claim ignorance from the language barrier.

"Thank you," I said sheepishly, dodging the critical looks from the tourist group who stood at least twenty feet away from the river's edge. I'd just demonstrated exactly what the guide had probably said *not* to do.

Then I realized Chase had just wrapped his arm around my body and practically carried me to safety, and my face flamed. I could still feel what remained of his touch on my skin. Those nerve endings would be wide awake for quite some time.

"You're welcome." His voice was still husky, as if he'd been truly, genuinely concerned.

"Wait—why are you here?" I asked, looking around. I didn't see any other Americans. He hadn't been on the bus with us, or I would have noticed.

"Someone said they saw you walking in the rain, but you weren't answering my texts or the radio. Since this is the only dead zone on the island, I came looking here first. Never thought you'd try to become some crocodile's dinner."

"Hey, they need to put some kind of fence up," I countered. "Anyone could make that mistake."

He paused. "Actually, that's true. You aren't the first. I'll have them put up a second sign closer to the bank. Not a fence though. The river is home to plenty of wildlife, and I don't want it disturbed."

I stared at him, remembering. "Right. You own the entire island."

His jaw tightened. "Not true. I purchased it from the investment company that originally built the resort, but this island is too beautiful to be owned by anyone, so I deeded it back to its residents. I prefer to think of myself as its caretaker. I screen tour groups before they come, and I limit new tourism projects from destroying the island's natural beauty. I have an understanding with those who live here. At least, as long as I own Everett Events and the resort."

Wow. So protective of the island he loved. "Do you have an understanding with the crocodiles too? I feel like you should."

He laughed.

I stared. I'd never seen Chase Everett laugh before.

"You never say what I expect, Daphne Porter," he said, his smile fading. "No, crocodiles play by their own rules. Still harmless compared to some of the monsters I work with in New York though."

I thought of Blythe and immediately frowned. She'd almost tanked his company to set herself up in the world, and here I stood—trusted with righting her wrongs and yet planning to tank his company the rest of the way. At least Blythe had done it behind Chase's back. She hadn't looked him in the eye every day and pretended to be something she wasn't.

Absently, I rubbed the place on my stomach where Chase had pulled me backward. "You said you were trying to reach me on the radio?"

"That's right. The police need a report from you about Kamia."

I groaned.

"It won't take long. Unless there's more you want to tell them. Perhaps a certain conversation you had with her that you'd like to keep on record, in case she decides to press charges against him later."

He knew about my conversation with Kamia in the cabana. Because of Marcus's accusations or because he had access to every resort worker within a five-mile radius? I couldn't forget how much power this man had.

"Got it," I said. "I'll tell them everything I know." Kamia would have wanted that.

I started for the bus, but Chase headed me off. "I brought my car. I'll give you a ride."

Moments later, I sat in the passenger seat of Chase Everett's car. I'd expected a corvette or luxury vehicle at the very least, but he drove a sporty black Subaru WRX-STI instead. It fit his personality better than anything else could have. Not that I could pay any attention to the car with Chase sitting just inches away. He gripped the wheel in a way that made his arms flex, his toned body filling the seat in a style that looked completely natural. Like this car was made for him. It even smelled like him. The edges of my consciousness felt a little fuzzy at the intoxication of it all.

"Nice ride," I told him, flinching at how shallow the words sounded.

"It's comfortable. I have another just like it in New York."

Interesting. I would have thought he'd use a limo or something. But no, I'd seen Chase walk into the lobby of Everett Events plenty of times. He never got dropped off out front. He had to be the only billionaire in the world who insisted on acting like he *wasn't* one.

"I didn't get a chance to thank you for what you did yesterday," I told him.

"Marcus deserved what he got. There's no excuse for a man to hurt someone more vulnerable. None." His tone was hard. Angry.

Something told me he wasn't even thinking about Marcus right now. "Was your uncle like that?"

"Worse. I'm only grateful he didn't have children. Better to live alone than with a man like him."

I couldn't remember Chase opening up like this before. It felt really good. For a moment, I allowed myself to forget Ty and my plans and that stupid fortune cookie and everything else. For now, I allowed myself to be what Chase needed.

"I'm sorry," I said softly. "For you and Kamia both. My adoptive parents have their issues, but at least I've always felt loved."

His eyes flicked to mine in an instant. "I didn't know you were adopted."

"Most people don't. I was four. My biological mom is serving a lifetime sentence in prison, and I've never felt a need to seek her out. My mom filled that role just fine." At least, until she'd looked at me right in the eye and lied about Dad. Until she'd broken my trust and made me feel like an outsider in my own home. My own town.

That day, I'd decided that if I had to be an outsider, I would do it on my own terms.

"Why this island?" I asked, sensing he didn't want to discuss family any longer.

He was silent for a long moment as the hotel came back into view. Pulling up under the resort lobby awning, Chase put the car into park and turned to face me.

"This island is the only place I've ever been happy," he said, his voice heavy. "And now I'm about to lose it forever."

TWELVE

THE NEXT MORNING, I didn't go to the hotel lobby because I was waiting for Ty. No, I had other reasons entirely—like counting the indoor palm trees and watching the janitor mop the shiny floor with a mop so dirty that it could only be making it worse and watching bleary-eyed families arrive with their restless and overtired children. One family had even brought their dog.

Each time a couple entered, my body reacted with a shot of adrenaline. After a couple of hours, my body felt so exhausted from the roller coaster ride of emotions that I felt an undeniable pull toward my bed.

Was I ready for this? Because I wasn't quite sure I was ready for this. Maybe I didn't have to see him today. His wedding wasn't for a week, and it wasn't like I could reveal myself the moment he set foot in the building without looking too eager. I had to bide my time, step in when the moment was right.

My mind made up, I stood and started to make my way

toward the back doors, throwing one last glance over my shoulder just in case. Then I froze mid-step.

Ty and his fiancée took up the entire double doorway when they entered. I barely recognized Ty with his khaki pants, sandals, and Hawaiian shirt—all clothes he wouldn't have been caught dead wearing before. But it was hard to miss Veronica. I'd never met her, obviously, but I recognized her from the tabloids. Tiny waist, almost boyish in stature, with a full chest that she showed off with a silk tank's plunging neckline. Even her chest screamed tanning bed. Her legs were so long, they seemed to go on forever, ending at cut-off Daisy Dukes. She'd dressed for a photo shoot, not an all-day airplane ride.

A man drew to a dead stop right in front of me, gaping. Then he leaned over to a second man. "That's Veronica Loyal."

"No way," the other breathed, squinting at her. Then he nodded. "Yeah, I think you're right. Who's the guy?"

"Must be that loser she's marrying this summer."

"She ain't married yet," said the second.

"She'll wish she was, the second she sees your ugly mug."

The other man punched the first in the shoulder, and they walked away laughing.

The resort staff hurried to help the couple with their bags and guided them toward the reception desk. I caught Ty's voice all the way across the lobby a few times and felt a sting of regret shoot through me. He sounded happy, relaxed.

What was I thinking?

I couldn't move. It felt like those nature shows where an owl stalked a fluffy bunny, and I rooted for the bunny while knowing it wouldn't end well...yet I still couldn't look away.

Soon the lovebirds headed in my direction. Their smiles immediately faded, and they started speaking in low tones, as if continuing an argument. It occurred to me too late that I had no idea how I wanted this to go. Did I want him to see me? Not to see me? Should I smile at him? Ignore him altogether?

They were closing in, and I had nowhere to run. So I whipped out my phone and pretended to be deep in conversation as they passed.

"There are things about this world you just don't understand, baby," Veronica was saying. "It's a nasty world sometimes. Luckily, you have me to guide you through it. All I'm asking is that you trust me until we start our life together..."

The timing went perfectly. I glanced up just as Ty caught sight of me, and we exchanged a look. A very long one. His eyes widened, his jaw went a little slack, and he gaped for a good three seconds.

Still holding the phone to my ear, I gave him a brilliant smile and a wave. This couldn't have gone better if I'd planned it.

Okay, I'd chosen my outfit carefully. Maybe the shirt plunged a little more than normal, and my skirt covered a little less skin than I was normally comfortable with. But I had one chance to wow Ty enough to make him wonder why he was with Veronica. The wondering would be incredibly important if I truly meant to steal him from her spiky clutches over the next week.

When I returned to my "office," I found my old Magic 8 ball tucked in the back of a drawer where I'd stuffed it days before. The still air was broken only by the sound of birds and the light drizzle of the island's usual afternoon rain. I wasn't sure why I'd brought this with me. A reminder of my purpose here? A token of the past?

I held the little black ball, took a deep breath, and asked, "Am I doing the right thing?" Then I gave it a series of hard shakes before angling the ball to await my results. *Come on, universe,* I pleaded silently. *Don't let me down.*

A triangular shape rotated in a blurry gray mass. Finally my answer appeared.

"Without a doubt," I read aloud, and felt my shoulders slump a little. Why did I feel a twinge of disappointment at the confirmation?

Fear of failure, perhaps. Or maybe discomfort at being "the pursuer," as my horoscope dictated. I wasn't used to chasing men, at least in the way I'd done today. Most of my relationships till now had been authentic and real.

And look where that got you, chided a voice from deep inside.

I glared at the Magic 8 ball and stuffed it back into its drawer. Then I turned back to my computer. I hadn't come to doubt my goal. I'd come to claim what was mine. To chase it, just like Cavil the cowboy chased his destiny. Ty had been wrong that fateful night. I knew what I wanted, and I wouldn't stop until I took it for my own.

My mission began now.

THIRTEEN

I STARED down at the pieces of harness in my hands, trying to figure out how it all fit together. The others made it look easy, stepping into the right holes and pulling it over to their chest. All I saw was a floppy piece of thick nylon and straps that looked like an ill-fitted horse halter. I picked a hole and stepped into it, but the hole next to it didn't seem to fit my other leg properly. Was it backwards?

A little more fiddling, and I stepped out and back in again, feeling it conform to my body. Now I had to tighten the darn thing. Remembering the expedition guide's instructions, I played with the buckle, but it wouldn't give. *Snug but not too tight.* But what did "too tight" mean, exactly? If I'd be dangling from the forest canopy a hundred feet over the ground, didn't I want it to be *really* tight so I didn't die?

I loved anything involving sports. I just wasn't so much into dangling high above the ground.

Why was I doing this again?

Chase had arranged this whole expedition as a complimentary surprise for the bride and groom, but I knew it had to be a desperate attempt to ensure the wedding went through. He hadn't said so, but I suspected he'd made the same deal with Ty and Veronica as Charles and Kamia. He wouldn't be taking any chances this time.

Chase met my helpless gaze, the slightest of smiles quirking at the edges of his lips. "May I?"

"I think this thing's trying to eat me," I growled.

"That happens to you a lot these days. It actually tightens right here." His strong hands gripped the harness and pulled it around my arms the correct way, then brought the pieces together and belted them in. A firm pull and the harness hugged my body more securely.

The back straps pushed on my butt in an odd way, but I'd get used to it. "Is it too loose?"

He stuck his fingers between the straps and my waist, barely brushing the back of my leggings and sending a warm tingle shooting down my body. If he noticed the touch, he didn't show it.

"No, it's perfect," he said. "Too tight and it'll cut off your circulation. That would make for a pretty miserable hour and a half."

I raised an eyebrow, trying not to show how much his accidental touch had affected me. "It takes an hour and a half to get down the mountain?"

"Sometimes longer if we have first-timers who brake a lot. This is one of the longest zip lines in the world."

Of course it was. Suddenly I wished I were sitting behind that desk back at the office, dealing with insignificant things like brides calling off weddings. Why had I chosen to stalk Ty on this particular excursion again? Even more importantly, how had I forgotten about my paralyzing fear of heights?

Chase leaned in. "Don't worry, we only lose tourists every other week. It's an off-week, so you're good."

I shot him a glare that he returned with a smirk before walking over to the guide and starting a whispered conversation.

I glanced over to Ty and Veronica, who already wore their harnesses and stood waiting. Veronica had a petite pout on her face, like a child who'd lost a battle and intended to sulk the rest of the afternoon. Her wavy blonde hair was piled on top of her head in a huge bun that seemed to defy the very elements. And Ty—

Ty looked at me. And frowned.

I yanked my gaze away, willing my cheeks not to blush. This was not the time to ogle over my target. This would be difficult enough with Chase watching my every move. Even now, as Chase spoke with the guide, his eyes flicked to me.

He seemed fine after the whole Kamia fiasco. As doomsday as his predictions had been about the company over the past couple of days, he didn't seem to have discussed it with anyone else. There hadn't been any whispers about the company tanking or financial woes. Maybe he'd exaggerated the issue. Regardless, the guy had billions, and that wasn't likely to change as a result of his wedding planner seizing her own happiness. I had to stop worrying about him and focus on the goal.

Operation Wedding Crash began now.

No, that was wrong. Operation Groom Stealer? Operation Groom...Retrieval. That didn't quite work either. Operation Boomerang?

"Let's go," the guide said and gestured to a bus that couldn't decide whether it was white or gray and looked to have survived World War II.

Ty pulled Veronica on before anybody else and made a beeline for the back of the bus. I tried to follow, but the tourist crowd pressed against the doorway, making it difficult to make any headway. When I finally made it on, there were only two seats left, right behind the driver and guide.

"After you," Chase said from behind me.

So much for casually chatting it up with Ty in the back. I slid against the window and waited as Chase sat next to me. I pressed against the patterned metal wall, putting as much space between my leg and his as possible. If he noticed, he didn't show it.

"That's eighteen," Chase told the driver. "We're good to go."

The bus started up, and we were on our way. The instant the bus lurched forward, my stomach lurched with it.

It would be just my luck if I came all this way to plummet to my death right in front of both the man I planned to marry *and* my boss.

Chase glanced at me several times over the next few minutes as the bus rounded a massive hill, climbing to the top while brushing past numerous tree branches. That certainly explained the missing paint on the bus's exterior, not that I could focus on the view with Chase watching me.

The guy had such a disorienting stare. Like he was trying to pry my own exterior apart and see what lay beneath, and he wouldn't be happy until he'd solved the mystery.

Finally, Chase leaned over. "I have motion sickness pills if you need a couple. They're stored in the back."

I looked at him in surprise. The second our eyes met, the full force of his gaze hit me like peering into the sun after dodging it many times before. It held an intensity that grabbed my attention and refused to release it. Did he approach everything in life this way, with such laser focus?

"I'm not motion sick," I managed, each word a struggle. "Why do you say that?"

"Because you're turning a darker shade of green by the minute. You aren't going to...?"

"No, no," I said quickly, a furious blush likely adding to the green tone of my skin. "Just a little worried. The guide said we'd be as high as a hundred feet above the ground."

"That's when we go over the valley. The rest of the canopy is closer to forty feet. But that only matters if you look down. The view is better if you look up anyway."

I'd managed to yank my gaze away, but at the term *Look up,* I found my eyes jerking back to his. A part of me had to admit that he was right—the view was pretty darn good. Chase's jaw flexed, emphasizing the stubble that he'd trimmed back but not eliminated completely. My fingers ached to run along his skin and feel the roughness there. His eyebrows were thick yet well-trimmed, framing dark brown eyes that looked brighter in the center. They reminded me of those pieces of amber on the dinosaur movie with the bugs inside.

Oh my gosh, Daphne, I chided myself. *You're such a nerd.*

"There's something I've been wondering," I said, the words coming out in a rush. "You don't need this. You could retire comfortably in New York without the company. Or here, even. So why do you care so much about keeping this company afloat?"

I instantly regretted the question when he tore his eyes away and looked forward again. It could have been my imagination, but his shoulders seemed to tense a bit.

"You don't have to answer that," I said, leaning against the window once more. "That's a pretty personal question."

"It is, but I'll answer it," he finally said. "Just not here. Later." His face turned slightly over his right shoulder, as if eyeing the tourists across the aisle and behind us.

"Of course." I tried to concentrate on the trees flashing by the window.

Just not here. Later. That sounded an awful lot like a conversation outside of work. The type of conversation between friends, not boss and employee.

Suddenly I felt far more nervous about that than anything else that lay ahead.

All too soon, I found myself hooked up to a zip line, standing on a high platform just beneath the thick forest canopy with a line of other people already zipping down. Ty and Veronica positioned themselves two couples in front of us, speaking in comfortable whispers, his hand around her waist or rubbing her arm or touching her whenever possible. The memory of his hands on me in exactly the same way, whispering things in my ear that he was likely whispering to her right now, made me want to punch her petite little face.

In a professional way, of course.

Several minutes into the wait, Ty looked backward and caught my gaze—and jerked it away with a guilty expression.

A surge of new hope filled my chest. Guilt was good. I could work with that. Soon we'd be leaving the island on a plane together, and it would be me he whispered sweet nothings to rather than preparing to career down a mountain with another woman.

I eyed my ring finger, empty as ever, and imagined the ring he would give me. Simple. Unique, like us. One of a kind with some kind of colored stone. We'd try on rings together—

Chase clipped in right behind me, and I was instantly aware of his presence. I'd know his musky scent in my sleep, recognize the feel of his eyes on me with my eyes closed. Ty made my stomach flutter...but Chase made every nerve in my body burn hot.

Curse Chase.

The line of tourists continued to throw themselves off the platform and down the line one after the other, some faster than others, many of them whooping in delight as they soared. When my turn came, I stared down at the forest floor that seemed a million miles below and felt a different kind of flutter in my stomach. My face had probably turned the same color as the forest.

My body froze up. Even if I wanted to step forward, I couldn't.

Chase drew even closer, whispering over my shoulder in a way that sent sparks shooting through my veins. "Keep your focus on the birds."

I almost wanted to pretend that I hadn't heard the first time so he'd do it again. My body practically shivered with the effect his whisper had against my ear. But instead, I remembered that this was my boss, and he only wanted us to make a good impression for the company's sake. It made the warmth fizzle somewhat.

Keep your focus on the birds.

Birds didn't congregate on the forest floor. They resided in the branches. I looked around and found one a few trees down, colorful and cheerful. Not worried at all about plummeting to its death. Just enjoying the beauty around us, living in the moment. Then it burst from the tree and soared high above the trees.

I channeled my inner child and pretended I was a bird. I lifted one of my arms like a wing, gripping the brake line with the other, and leaped.

My stomach wrenched upward for a second as the line took my weight.

Then I was flying.

The world around me slowed. The forest was a greenish blur, the sky an endless blue. The crisp air sweeping past. My inner child rose up from within in an uncontrollable fit of giggles. Pure happiness.

I got it now.

I lifted both hands like an eagle lifting off and soaring to the sky. I felt more awake, more alive, than ever before. A gleeful whoop tore from my lips. The bird darted alongside me, flapping its wings happily.

The platform came into view ahead, and I remembered that I was supposed to slow. I put pressure on the line and then panicked a bit as it didn't decelerate right away. The worker on the platform, his eyes wide, cupped his hands around his mouth and called, "Brake!"

At the very last second, I slowed enough to stumble onto the platform with the others. I stood there, triumphant and invigorated and grinning like a complete fool. "That. Was. Incredible."

Ty chuckled. I saw the same excitement in him that I felt in myself. "Right?"

Veronica pouted. "It's not incredible. It's boring. I want to go back to the beach."

A zipping sound grew louder, reminding me that Chase was right behind me and had probably seen the whole thing. Strangely, I didn't care. I felt as though I'd unlocked something deep inside that I didn't know was there. Like a video game level-up.

The second Chase arrived—much more gracefully than I had, admittedly—he started clapping his gloved hands. There was an unusual light dancing in his eyes. Amusement?

"Well done," he said. "Not bad for a first time. Just brake a little sooner on this next one."

I frowned. "I like going fast."

"I do too, but smacking into a tree at 30 miles per hour doesn't feel good." He flinched.

I nudged him playfully with my shoulder. "Chase Everett. Are you speaking from experience?"

His embarrassment grew. I loved the look of it. "Possibly. The worst part was, I was upside down. It's a good thing my instructor forced me to wear a helmet, or it could have been a lot worse."

I gaped at him. "You can go *upside down*?"

"Of course." His eyes twinkled. "Want to try it?"

"Duh!"

His eyes crinkled in confusion, and I realized I'd just said "Duh" to the billionaire. My inner child apparently wanted to take over completely today.

I kind of wanted to let her.

"You can even go upside down and backwards," Ty piped in. "I can show you, Daphne, if you want."

Chase rounded on him. "I don't recommend that here. It's too fast, and we don't have stop blocks until the bottom."

Ty scowled. "I've done it a zillion times, all over the world. I'll be fine."

"You're getting married in a few days," Chase reminded him. "Doesn't seem like a time to be taking chances like that. The last thing we need is a spinal injury or concussion to deal with."

"Ty," Veronica said, looking worried. "He's right."

Ty glared at her. "I was a guide in Hawaii for a whole summer. I know what I'm doing."

"I'm sure you do, but it isn't just about you now. It's about us. Let's not take risks today." She batted her eyes and turned the pout-meter up to a 10.

"It isn't a risk," Ty snapped, his voice rising in volume. "Look, I'll show you."

"This one's too steep," Chase said. "If you insist on it, try run 11 where it's more level."

"I'm not waiting that long. You people worry too much, okay? It's super easy."

Veronica's hand grabbed his wrist. "Chase knows this run, and we should trust him. Show me on 11. Okay?"

Ty glared at her, looking frustrated. I could tell he wanted to please her, but this wasn't about Veronica at all.

This was about me.

"Ty," Chase said, trying once more. "If you wait till 11, there's an extra worker there who can capture your run on video. I'll radio her right now and give her the heads up. I'm sure all of YouTube would love to see that."

Veronica clapped her gloved hands together. "We can put it on our wedding video!"

Ty grumbled something under his breath and reclaimed his hand, turning back to the run and the worker watching him with wide eyes. The man finally nodded and Ty pushed off, picking up speed by the second as he disappeared into the forest canopy. Veronica followed the second the worker allowed it, barely giving us a glance.

Chase sighed. "Tourists." He unhooked his cable and stepped in front of me, clipping it back in and adjusting a couple of things.

"Wait," I said. "You're still going upside down? I thought it was too steep."

"Not for me. I could do this course in my sleep and blindfolded. You just have to have an awareness of how close you are to the end, which Ty doesn't. Now you'll take off like before, but then you'll arch your back and let your head hang low. Watch." He started off the platform. Within seconds, he swung around, his helmet scraping the branches below. Just when I thought he would right himself, he swung his arms wide and let himself pick up speed.

It looked exhilarating.

"Go ahead," the worker on the platform said. It sounded a lot like "It's your funeral."

Then I remembered the concern in Chase's eyes when he'd pulled me away from the crocodiles. That event had scared him. This one did not. He wouldn't let me get hurt.

Unlike Ty, who had shattered my heart once and walked away. The thought bothered me more than I wanted to admit.

"Hi, ho, and away!" I shouted, leaping off the platform once again. I spread my arms and reveled in that falling-speeding-flying feeling once again before taking a deep breath and arching my back. It felt like falling for a short second, then the world turned on its head, and the sky was green and the ground blue. The branches whipped past, closer to my face than ever, and the birds chirped their approval.

I felt like letting go would make me fall, so I made myself do it to conquer this last fear. My arms spread, I suddenly felt like a superhero flying through a city of leaves.

"Brake!" a voice called from in front of me.

Oh, right. The platform. I tried to pull myself up but couldn't.

Crap.

I managed to grab hold of the brake line and apply pressure, slowing me a bit, but the platform was still approaching way too fast. Grabbing hold of my harness with the other hand, I gave one last massive effort to heave myself upward—

And felt a set of powerful arms catch me.

My momentum stopped in an instant, and I found myself enveloped by Chase Everett. All of him. Every inch of him on every inch of me, and him all around, and the world was no longer green and blue or up and down but *him*.

"You," he said, his voice husky, "are insane."

I should have been horrified—the guy had saved me yet again, after all—but instead, I felt more alive than ever in my life. I lifted my face and laughed, completely free.

He didn't seem angry. Instead, it was concern again and maybe a little bit of something more. That little bit of something may have had something to do with the fact that his arms were still wrapped around me protectively.

My uncontrollable laughter slowed and turned into a soft chuckle, muffled against his hard chest and the powerful scent of musk, tree leaves, and peppermint. The zip line was fun, but this—*this* was exhilaration like I'd never experienced before. I wanted to stay here in his arms forever. My insides ignited like a forest fire.

Even more strangely, I saw that same exhilaration mirrored in his own eyes. Seconds passed, and he didn't look away. Not once. There he stood, looking stricken, like someone had punched him in the face, yet wanting to experience the sensation again and again.

Someone cleared his throat across the platform, tearing my gaze back to reality.

Ty stared at us with a dark expression, his eyes narrowed in a combination of hurt and betrayal. Then he launched off the platform once more.

FOURTEEN

I DIDN'T SEE Ty the rest of the day. Thankfully, I had plenty to keep me busy. Less than an hour after arriving back at the office following the zip lining excursion, the florist came to my office in a panic. An entire shipment of florals had been loaded onto the wrong plane and shipped off to Nicaragua. She and I spent two hours making phone calls—to the airline, the insurance agency, and other florists within an hour of here.

The moment we'd found a local company able and willing to supply this weekend's shipment on time and the florist had left wiping her tears, the cake decorator's husband called with the news that she'd been admitted to the hospital with kidney failure and would be out for the foreseeable future.

Growling, I scrambled to thumb through Blythe's old files on local cake decorators and found nothing. I was literally doing a search on my laptop for nearby cake decorators when a bride called and said she'd forgotten her shoes and could I find a replacement pair? Because ivory silk sandals in size 6 were easy to find on the island, of course.

By the time the photographer texted with the news that

he'd broken an expensive lens on today's photo shoot and would need an advance so he could replace it, I wanted to pull my hair out and light everything on fire...and then light the fire on fire.

Yet despite it all, I felt skilled for the first time since arriving here. Blythe had taken care of most of the details up till now. Finally, I had something that needed my attention, and mine alone. I'd tackled every single problem with my signature Daphne stubbornness until a solution presented itself. Me, not Blythe.

On some deep level, I kind of loved it.

I was swatting my fiftieth mosquito when a knock sounded on the corner of the open wall, just before Chase emerged from the shadows and into the dim light. He looked around. "It's 10:00 p.m. What are you still doing here?"

10? Could it really be that late? I sighed. "Just putting out a few fires."

"I heard about the flowers. Somebody's getting fired over that."

Stiffening, I stared at him.

He seemed puzzled by my reaction before understanding. "Somebody at the airline," he clarified. "Not...here. Not you. It wasn't your fault."

Chase looked strangely unsettled tonight. It occurred to me that my boss was here, in my office, incredibly late and alone. Had I done something wrong today? Did this have something to do with his showing off on the zip line? Maybe he felt guilty for the unprofessional nature of it all. But he'd left his stern demeanor at home tonight. This man looked somewhat normal —tired and a little flustered. What could have gotten him this rattled?

"Thanks," I said carefully. "Is there something I can help you with?"

"I'm wondering something." The words came out in a rush before dying completely in a pool of silence.

He still stood across the room and I sat in my office chair, so I motioned to the hard sofa in front of my desk. "Do you want to sit?"

"No." He ran a hand over his hair, then seemed to notice the gesture and shoved it into his pocket instead.

Oh. The guy almost seemed *nervous*. This couldn't be good.

"Come on a walk with me," he finally said.

A walk. With Chase Everett. Like two normal people, shooting the breeze. "Is something wrong?" I asked, rising to my feet.

"No." He headed for the open wall and the outdoors without another word.

Okay? "Let me lock up here. I'll head home afterward." I placed Blythe's scattered papers back into the file before heading over to close the open wall.

He nodded curtly. "I'll walk you home then."

Once everything was locked up, we started walking in silence, the night sky above freckled with a smattering of stars. They didn't look regular and tidy at all. These were beautiful in their messiness, natural and clumping and varying in brightness and color. Kind of like people. The very best ones, at least.

Meanwhile, here Chase stood, walking with his hand just inches from mine. He wore a loose golf polo and fitted trousers with his sunglasses pulled up onto his head, for once. If I didn't know who he was, I never would have guessed this man had such incredible wealth. What would it be like, harboring more money than you knew what to do with? Would I work as hard as he did, running all over the island and trying to make people happy?

Nah. I'd retire on an island exactly like this one and pay people to make *me* happy.

"You said you had a question," I prodded after two full minutes of silence.

He drew in a sharp breath as if I'd startled him. "I shouldn't ask. It's really none of my business."

Now he had my full attention. "You're wondering something about me?"

"Yes. Well, about Ty today. He couldn't keep his eyes off you." He fixed me with a probing stare. "Do you two know each other?"

Triple crap. Quadruple crap? I couldn't remember what number I'd reached at this point. All that mattered was my boss was suspicious about Ty and me, and this could all end tonight if I wasn't careful.

I chose my words as precisely as a gymnast walking on a balance beam. "We went out a few times in New York, but it didn't work out. Please tell me you aren't worried about my stealing the groom."

"No." He stepped in front of me, blocking my path and forcing me to look up into his shadowed eyes. "I'm more worried about the groom stealing my wedding planner."

He didn't look angry. Only concerned. No, not even that— almost anxious, maybe even a little jealous.

A pleasant shiver darted through my body, one far stronger than the one I'd felt upon first seeing Ty yesterday. I shouldn't feel this way in Chase's presence. For one thing, boss-employee relationships never worked out well. For another thing, we were alone on this path on an island he owned—this could end up all kinds of inappropriate. And for a last thing...

I would soon be betraying Chase Everett. Getting close to him first wouldn't be smart.

Swallowing hard, I stepped around him and continued

walking. "Well, this wedding planner happens to like her job. Besides, that was a long time ago."

"At least seven months ago, I would guess, because that's how long he and Veronica have been dating." He took a deep breath. "I know, because before that, she was dating me."

I'm pretty sure my jaw dropped about a second later, because I found myself standing on that path, positively gaping. "You...and Veronica?"

"I know. We weren't exactly made for each other, which is why it didn't last longer than a few weeks. I ended things when I realized commitment meant different things to each of us." He scowled.

I didn't know what to say. Chase and Veronica *did* make more sense than Veronica and Ty. But the fact that he would ask her out even once made me feel strangely disappointed. Was Veronica more his type? Did he seek out others in his same social class regularly?

Of course he did. Who else would a billionaire date? *Come on, Daphne. Get it together.* I wanted Ty, not Chase. If I had to repeat that a thousand times before it would sink in, I would do it.

"Why are you telling me this?" I asked.

Chase stopped pacing and looked directly at me. "I think Ty and Veronica's wedding is a sham."

This conversation had only gotten stranger by the minute. "Seriously? Why?"

"Veronica won't stop seeking me out. Everywhere I go, she's there. I feel like I'm being haunted by the ghost of girlfriends past." He grimaced. "I think she's trying to make me jealous."

I stumbled over a tree root and tried to play it cool. "Really."

"There's no other reason she would hire my company. Veronica is clever and conniving, so there's a reason for everything she does. That's where you come in, Daphne. I want you to pretend to be my girlfriend."

If Chase had sprouted horns, I wouldn't have been more dumbfounded. "Girlfriend?" I mentally kicked myself at how ridiculous I sounded right now, echoing everything he said, but my brain simply couldn't process this.

"If you and I are dating—pretending to date, anyway—she'll leave me alone and hopefully go through with the wedding. And if Ty harbors old feelings for you, which I suspect is the case, this will solve that problem too."

He must have seen my dazed expression, because he stepped closer, forcing me to look upward, and lowered his voice.

"It's only a few days, but Daphne, you don't have to do this. It isn't a work assignment. This is a friend asking a friend for a favor."

Chase Everett saw me as a friend.

The realization felt like a bucket of ice water over my head. If only he knew what lies and betrayals I harbored in my sick little heart.

This plan of his paralleled my own in many ways. It would be far easier to make Ty jealous if Chase was in on it too. But fake dating could possibly do too thorough a job and drive Ty away, just like Chase said. And if he was right about Veronica believing the ruse and going through with the wedding, wasn't that the opposite of what I wanted?

It came down to a single fact—I had no other plan. Fake dating seemed risky and it could ruin everything, but it also had the potential to do exactly what I wanted. There was only one way to know. If things went wrong, I could always tell Chase I didn't feel comfortable continuing.

But if I did succeed in running away with Ty, Chase would be devastated. He'd chosen me for this because he trusted me.

A friend, he'd said. The more time I spent with Chase, the harder it would be to do what needed to be done.

"I don't want to hurt anyone," I whispered.

Chase waved it off. "Veronica will be fine, and so will Ty. But I know this is kind of an unorthodox request, so don't feel like I'm pressuring you. It's your decision. You keep your job either way, and I trust you."

I trust you.

"You should know that I'm not really a fancy dress kind of girl," I said quickly, before the guilt could fully hit. "I'm sure there's another employee who could be more convincing in that department."

Chase shook his head. "We've been seen together several times since your arrival. Nobody will question us. A few days, Daphne, and then we can pretend to break up and you'll be free again."

He'd pried every argument from my determined fists, and now I felt stripped bare. "Fine, but I have one condition. There can't be any kissing."

His lips pressed together as if stifling a laugh. "Why's that?"

"Kissing is real, and this is not. I don't want any confusion between us." Chase would already be crushed by my stealing Ty. I didn't want him accusing me of manipulating him, not even with something as simple as a kiss.

Besides, the thought of kissing Chase lit an odd fire deep inside. If the thought of his lips pressed against mine made me feel like this, what would a real kiss do? I shuddered at the thought, but not in a bad way. Yep. Definitely needed a kissing ban.

"No kissing *without* permission," Chase confirmed, and his addition gave my heart a little thrill. "Our first event is the Hall-strom-Benedict reception tomorrow night. I've invited Ty and

Veronica so they can make a few last-minute decisions. I look forward to seeing you there." He held my gaze as he spoke, and his eyes contained all the confidence in the world. He really did trust me. In many ways, the welfare of his company relied on this. Maybe more, given what he'd said about losing his island.

"I'll do my best," I replied numbly.

Even as I said it, I felt the betrayal of the words in my very bones.

FIFTEEN

As Chase had predicted, everything came together just fine for the reception the next evening. I'd been tempted to send him a text about needing to skip the reception to take care of a few things, but I knew Chase would only hunt me down. So I took extra care styling my hair and applying evening eye shadow, something I rarely did. I slid into my only formal gown, a form-fitting deep gray dress with a high side slit and plunging neckline from five years ago. Thankfully it still fit—this island had definitely kept me active.

Styling my hair into a quick chignon to get the hair off my neck, I gave myself one last look. Then I pulled a few wisps of hair around my face, cheeks warming at the overall effect. Which man did I want to impress most? I couldn't say, and that made my heart pound harder than it had in a long time.

When I arrived at the event, I was grateful to find everything in order down to the tiniest flower. The florist had outdone herself tonight. A quartet played in the corner, their tuxes not a millimeter out of place. The guests all appeared to be in Chase's social class, because I saw no lack of expensive clothing and jewelry. Fitted gowns, fitted tuxes, fit bodies. Couples swaying to the music with careful smiles. It looked like a movie set.

Chase stood near the doorway. When he spotted me, his eyes widened a bit and ran the length of my body, which I immediately forgave him for. The guy hadn't seen me in anything but casual clothes and white work polos since my arrival.

He made his way over and halted a foot away, arms folded. "You look . . ." His voice broke. "You look beautiful."

"Thank you." I sighed. "Okay, first of all, nobody will believe we're dating when you stand like a soldier at attention. You looked more believable yesterday at the zip line course."

Chase's shoulders instantly relaxed, and the edges of his lips quirked. He leaned in to whisper, and I could feel his warm breath on my bare neck, making my breath hitch. "That's because I thought I'd killed you, sending you sailing down that line upside down on your second run."

"It'll take more than that to finish me off." I caught a glimpse of Ty and Veronica entering through the north doors. "Ready for this?"

He cleared his throat. "I should have thought this through. I can't touch you, being your boss. My lawyer would have me drawn and quartered. I didn't even write up a contract, and we have no understanding of what contact is appropriate and what isn't . . ."

As Chase rambled on, Ty caught sight of me and stopped in his tracks, pulling Veronica to a halt beside him.

I slid my arm beneath Chase's and rounded his waist, liking how his arm wrapped easily around me and mindful of several pairs of watching eyes. "It's fine," I whispered. "I promise not to sue over something that isn't even real."

His jaw closed with an audible snap as Ty and Veronica

approached, my ex practically stalking across the dance floor. His cheeks were the same color as yesterday while zip lining, and there was fire in his eyes. Next to me, Chase cocked an eyebrow.

"Beautiful event," Veronica said when they arrived. "So sweet of you, Chase, to invite us to this reception so we could see how ours will go. I love how you're going to so much trouble to make our wedding special."

On the surface, she seemed genuine enough. The glint of anger in her eyes was the only indication of the poison beneath her words.

I rested my head against Chase's shoulder. If anything, he went even stiffer at the contact, but I pretended not to notice. "He knows how to throw a party," I cooed, echoing the sultry nature of Veronica's voice. "There's a reason he has the clientele he does. Right, honey?"

"Right," Chase said, sounding strangled.

"We all know who deserves the praise," Ty broke in. "Everything will be exactly how we wanted it, down to the black and white theme with red roses. Veronica is very pleased, and it takes a lot to please her." His fiancée jerked and glared at him, but he continued smoothly, ignoring us both. "If our wedding is this elaborate, I can only imagine how expensive yours will be. Assuming this whole thing works out, of course."

I saw his motives in an instant. Ty was fishing for information, testing the strength of our relationship.

"Of course," I agreed evenly. "If it happens, we want our wedding to take place here too. Except it won't be extravagant at all. Simple, actually."

"Oh?" Veronica's voice sounded nearly as tight as Chase's. "In what way?"

"The entire island would be invited," Chase broke in. "Open to anyone who wanted to attend. And everyone would be barefoot for the ceremony, a line of people standing in the sand."

In an instant, the scene surrounded us. I could feel the ocean wind in my hair, the salty sea air caressing me, the soft sand between my toes, and Chase's hand in mine.

Wait. No. My dream was of holding *Ty's* hand. Marrying him in Four Seasons Park in New York, or even the courthouse, for that matter. As long as I won him back from Veronica, it wouldn't matter where the wedding took place.

But the wedding Chase described felt so blasted *right*.

The quartet's jazzy number paused and a new one began, softer and slower this time.

Chase leaned over, his palm sliding down my bare arm and taking hold of my hand. It sent a wave of heat down my entire body. I was surprised Ty and Veronica couldn't feel it. "Would you like to dance, my dear?" he whispered.

"Love to," I managed.

"Aw, you guys are so cute," Veronica said, her eyes shooting daggers that screamed the opposite. "So happy for you, Chase."

"And I for you." Chase placed his hand on my back and guided me through the crowd and toward the dance floor. I felt Veronica's eyes boring into my back as he turned to face me, bringing my hands to his shoulders.

My brain fled altogether. I'd have to avoid intelligent conversation in Chase's presence for the next few days or risk being outed.

Outed as what? something deep inside asked. *Attracted to Chase?*

It was a good question. Nearly every woman in this room watched him now, one of the world's most eligible bachelors in the center of the ballroom floor on a tropical island. What did they think when seeing us together? A billionaire boss and his newest employee? A tailored man and a frumpy woman whose dress hadn't quite gotten de-wrinkled and whose hair was poofing out from humidity? Easy competition? Temporary like all the others?

I am temporary, I reminded myself. It didn't get much more temporary than a few days.

Chase's hands slid around my waist, and he pulled me in close. If my back had felt warm before, now my entire body burned like a bonfire.

"They're coming over," Chase murmured against my ear, sending pleasant tingles down my neck.

"This is one of her favorite songs," Ty explained when he arrived, as if feeling the need to explain their sudden dart across the dance floor.

Veronica scowled at him. "You know I can do my own talking, right? Is this how you're going to be?"

"What do you mean? I'm just being myself."

"No, you're not. You're being weird."

"I'm not being weird."

"Yes, you are. Ever since we got here and you saw someone you knew in the lobby. You ever going to tell me who that was?" Veronica's eyes could have drilled a hole through Ty's face had he been looking at her. Instead, his eyes were fixed on me in Chase's arms.

"It was nobody," Ty growled.

"Don't you lie to me," Veronica snapped. "Tell me the truth, or I'm walking out of here now."

I knew exactly who that person was, and so did Ty. But to his credit, he turned to the woman he planned to marry with nothing but sincerity in his gaze. "I swore never to lie to you, and I'll keep that promise. I thought I saw a woman I dated a long time ago. But my eyes were playing tricks on me, because it wasn't her. And it wouldn't have mattered if it were, because

I have you now. You're incredible, my everything. Together, *we're* everything."

I'd pulled slightly away from Chase to overhear the conversation next to us, so I forced myself back into his arms before Ty could notice.

Veronica cocked her head. "Aw, Tycie. You sure she isn't on the island, then?"

"Baby, she isn't even on the same planet as you."

Smooth, Ty. Very smooth.

Chase swore under his breath, barely loud enough for me to hear. It pulled my attention back to him. "What?" I whispered.

His eyes were full of mischief. "I don't want to be on whatever planet those two are on."

I threw back my head and laughed before I could help it. The tight grip he'd held on his smile slipped a bit at my reaction, making me laugh even harder.

It gave me great satisfaction to note that Ty watched us both as he cradled his fiancée, his eyes positively blazing.

I recognized that look. It was the expression he'd worn right before launching a baseball into a catcher's mitt and winning a league game two years ago. He'd also worn that look one night after losing an important court case, a rare occurrence for him, before picking up the phone to ask—no, demand—that the client let him file an appeal. He'd won the appeal by sheer iron will and the persistence of a toddler with his eyes on the blue cup rather than the green one.

Whatever Ty wanted, he got.

And now, more than ever, he wanted me.

SIXTEEN

Early the next morning, I was going over the inventory and staff lists for a third time when a text arrived about a staff sand volleyball game at 10 a.m. I'd considered spending most of the day stalking Ty, but the text contained a very important word. One I couldn't resist.

Volleyball. I hadn't played in way too long.

Thoughts of Chase leaped into my mind. Would he be there?

I tried to imagine the guy running around, hurtling himself at a ball before it hit the ground, and laughed. Nope. He seemed like a sidelines-and-taking-pictures kind of guy. Probably a good thing, because I tended to get competitive at these things.

I reached the sand volleyball courts only five minutes late, but the rest of the wedding staff had already started playing. I stripped my shirt and skirt off to reveal my deep purple bikini and left my denim shorts on. They'd constrict my movement slightly, but the last thing I needed right now was a wardrobe malfunction that included my butt hanging out for all to see.

To my surprise, Chase was here too. He'd made himself captain of one team and Agwe captain of the other.

Even more to my surprise, he'd taken his shirt off and stood just in front of the net, the usual sunglasses covering his piercing eyes and his skin glistening ever so slightly. Sunscreen? Tanning oil? Perspiration? I'd have to touch him to know...and I *really* wanted to touch him right now.

It wasn't my fault. He looked like a swim suit model. Seriously. The guy must spend hours in the gym every day. He didn't seem like the protein shake-guzzling, egg-swallowing, weightlifter type. Then again, he hadn't seemed like the sand volleyball type either. But who would have thought that under his stuffy suit and tie, Chase Everett would look like that? And tanned, no less.

The ball sailed over the net, just beyond Chase's reach. He leaped backward, got his fingers under it, and managed to lob it into the sky before landing in the soft sand. A woman I didn't recognize tried to get it over the net but failed. The others laughed, and a guy stepped forward to offer Chase a hand out of the sand pile that currently held him captive. Without hesitation, he accepted it and rose to his feet, brushing off his glistening skin that now held patches of rough sand.

He took his place at the net and paused, turning to catch my gaze. I couldn't see what lay behind those sunglasses, but I did note how his lips parted slightly as he took me in. I could practically feel his gaze sweep over my body as his smile froze.

He wasn't the only one looking at me now. Both teams stared. I'd forgotten that Ty and Veronica weren't the only ones who'd seen us together last night. The "news" was officially out now, and I'd be using my best acting skills for the foreseeable future.

"Hey," Chase said, coming over to give me a hug. He

planted a light kiss on the top of my head. Even that sent a jolt down my body clear down to the sand.

"Daphne," Agwe called in his accented English. He wore a knowing grin. "Join us. We are shorter."

I hid a smile, knowing what he meant. I trotted over and gave my new teammates a high five as Chase took his previous spot once more. In an instant, I snapped into competition mode. The eight years since high school trickled away, leaving only focus and determination.

The game began. One serve after another got picked up by the wind and thrown out of bounds. Occasionally we'd return the ball and rotate. Soon I found myself face-to-face with Chase.

Standing here, my feet buried in sand, he seemed larger than life and completely in his element. I hadn't realized he was so competitive. Clearly the guy had plenty of experience on the court. Maybe even as much as I did.

"Game point," he said.

I realized he was talking to me. All I could see in his dark glasses was my reflection. It made me sweep a hand over my messy hair. "We're only seven points behind. It's been known to happen."

"Possible, yes. Likely? No."

I gave him a smirk before turning to find Agwe stepping up to the serving line. "Go, Agwe!" I called. "You've got this."

The man leaped into the air and slammed the ball, sending it sailing over the net. The ball found its target between two members of Chase's team and hit the sand before anyone could touch it.

Oh. He really did have this.

"Six," I said.

Chase only smiled.

Two more serves, each in a different location across the

court, and Chase's team looked a little less cocky than before. Even Chase's smile had faded.

On the fourth serve, someone managed to bump the ball upward, and Chase tipped it over the net.

Acting instinctively, I dove and got my fingers under it, propelling it back into the sky. Sand flew behind me as Agwe hurried to set the ball, allowing another man to spike it. He'd been careful to send it out of Chase's reach, and it paid off. The woman next to Chase made a dig and sent it sailing out of bounds before it could reach the net.

"Three," I said to Chase, whose frown had deepened. "Care for a friendly wager, *sweetie?*"

One trimmed eyebrow lifted. "Name your terms."

"If my team wins, I get your sunglasses."

He looked genuinely taken aback. "You want my aviators?"

"Not really, but I think that'll make you play worse next game. Now name *your* terms."

He snickered. "*When* my team wins, you accompany me on an errand in town later."

I paused, trying to figure out why he would possibly want me tagging along. "What kind of errand?"

"Not telling. Take it or leave it."

The entire court was listening now, I saw.

I feigned nonchalance with a casual shrug. "Sure? As long as your errand doesn't include crocodiles."

"I make no guarantees. Last chance to back out, darling."

"Bring it on."

I turned and grinned at Agwe, who watched us both with a strange expression. When I nodded, he snapped back into his groove. With a leap that shouldn't have been possible in sand, he slammed the ball over the net. It flew over Chase's head, landing barely within bounds before anyone could dive for it.

"Two," I sang.

"We know how to count," Chase growled. He dug his feet into the sand, swung his arms, and settled in to watch Agwe, every muscle tense. He looked like a wolf about to spring. I saw myself reflected in his sunglasses, a pale blur of a reflection. I made a mental note to get a little more sun this summer.

Agwe called out the score, lifted the ball, and pitched it over the net—only to groan as it sailed slightly too far to the right. Luckily, a woman in her forties leaped up at the last second and tipped it into the net. It bounded right back at her and hit the sand.

My team and I cheered, gave each other high fives, and took our places once more. Adrenaline pumped through my system. I tried not to think about how I would be winning either way— I'd get Chase's aviators or a date with him in town.

Not a real date.

Not a date.

Very much *not*—

I watched Chase as the slap of a new serve sounded behind me. The ball sailed over the net. This time, it headed dead center in Chase's court. His team surged into action—a man bumped it, a woman gave a perfect set, and Chase leaped as if in slow motion.

His arm swept backward as he flew through the air with perfect form, preparing to launch.

I leaped to the net and jumped, my arms rigidly in the air, fingers splayed.

Chase's hand made contact with the ball before I could even blink—

—and I found myself lying on the ground, staring at the vast expanse of blue sky overhead and tasting sand and blood.

What the . . . ?

Chase's face appeared, worry etched into his expression. I felt pressure on my hand and realized he was holding it.

"...so sorry," he was saying amidst the ringing in my ears. "I got too into it. That was stupid. Are you okay?"

I yanked my hand from his and touched my face. Warm stickiness covered my fingers. A bloody nose.

This could not be happening.

"It's not serious," the woman who'd missed the ball earlier said, kneeling at my other side. "She should probably be evaluated for a concussion, though, just in case. I'll take her to the resort nurse so you can finish the game."

"No. I've got her." Chase's hands slid beneath me, and then the heated sand disappeared, replaced by cooler air and slightly calloused fingers and a warm, hard chest against my ribs.

The woman frowned. "I have medical training. I'll get her there safe and sound."

Chase's voice boomed in his chest next to my head. "There's nobody here she'll be safer with than me." Then the world turned and we were on our way.

Chase Everett was carrying me.

On a tropical island.

Shirtless.

And I wore a bikini...*oh.*

I looked downward to ensure I was covered in the right places. Thankfully, my swimsuit still fit correctly. At least I hadn't gotten knocked out while my swimsuit flew into the sunset in front of my entire work team. That would have been infinitely worse.

I used my free arm to wipe my nose. It didn't seem as bad as they'd all made it out to be. "I can walk just fine." With my nose still gushing, it sounded more like *I cad walk just fide.*

"I'm sure you can. This is just a precaution." He didn't seem winded at all.

"That was a rather dramatic exit. If anyone wondered before, you may have convinced them about us."

His eyes fell on me, direct and unwavering. "Even if we weren't pretending, do you really think I'd send you with Suzanne after smashing your nose with a volleyball?"

I couldn't answer that. The man I'd known before this week absolutely would have. But now everything felt muddled and confusing, like a nest of tangled yarn. "You'd have every right."

His jaw tightened, but he said nothing more the rest of the way.

SEVENTEEN

"HERE YOU GO," the medical assistant said, holding the door for me. I slipped through and into the lobby where Chase still waited. He'd found a shirt somewhere, or maybe he'd made a quick trip back to his room in the past forty minutes.

I thanked her and headed to the reception desk, but Chase shook his head. "It's already been taken care of. I'll walk you home."

I glanced at the receptionist, who watched us with the sharpness of a mother hen. "Not home. We have an errand in town, remember?"

His eyes flicked to the woman, then back. "You need to rest."

"Chase," I said firmly. "It was a bloody nose. I'll be a little sore, but it's not a big deal."

"No concussion?"

"None. Not even worth the hundred bucks or whatever you just paid."

"Worth a thousand times that to make sure you're okay." He nodded to the receptionist, who barely inclined her head back, and held the door as we went outside. "I'm calling off that stupid bet."

"Too late. I'd say you won pretty decisively. It's a shame I won't get those aviators though." I looked down at my bikini top. "I should probably find my shirt."

"I grabbed you one from the gift shop." He tossed me a wadded-up piece of cloth.

I opened it up and brushed the fabric, which was covered in sequins that spelled out ISLE DE PURA VIDA.

"They didn't have any others in your size," Chase said.

I didn't question how he knew my size. Slipping the shirt over my head to hide the coming blush, I nodded in approval. "At least the crocodiles will see me coming a mile away."

"You sure you don't want to go home and rest?" he asked when we reached the outdoors.

"No. I mean, yes, I'm sure. Tomorrow is too busy, so it has to be today." I swept my hair over my shoulder, wishing I knew where my hairband had gone. Probably in that pile of sand somewhere.

"You still have sand in your hair." He reached up and gently swept a hand along the back of my head—quickly at first, then softly and slowly combing through my hair with his fingers.

They say hair doesn't have nerves, but I swear his touch sent electricity shooting down to my toes.

"It's fine," I said, turning to break contact and look directly at him.

When he saw my slightly bruised nose, he flinched and cupped my face in his hands, brushing my cheek with his thumb. His touch was so gentle, I could barely feel it—yet it still sent tingles along the surface of my skin. "I'm such an idiot," he said softly.

"I mean, possibly. Or maybe I bring out your Olympic-level

volleyball skills." I took his hands and lowered them from my face. It could have been my imagination, but his breath seemed to hitch slightly. "If you really want to repay me, let's walk to town instead of driving. It's too beautiful outside."

His mouth curved into a slow smile. "I have a better idea."

Minutes later, I found myself hugging Chase from behind, the wind whipping past us on his motorcycle as we weaved along the narrow palm-lined road. Not as fast as I would have driven if given the chance though. Chase drove carefully, deliberately, as if worried to go a single kilometer above the speed limit. He'd given me the helmet yet looked completely unaffected by the wind behind his beloved aviators.

When we reached the main road and parked, I slid only a few inches before Chase turned and grabbed my arm, helping me stand. Had he held on a moment too long, or did he simply feel guilty and overprotective because of the volleyball incident?

He hooked the helmet around his handlebars, and we started to saunter along the sidewalk.

"Where are we headed?" I asked. The town looked busy, but not as busy as the first day I'd driven through. Maybe midday was slower here, like in many Latin American countries. "And why is my presence necessary for this incredibly important errand in town?"

"I keep my promises" was all he'd say.

We walked for a full five minutes, taking in all the details of one of the most charming island towns I'd ever set foot in, before either of us spoke.

"I think if there was an opposite of New York, this would be it," I said.

Chase turned to examine me. "Is that a good thing or a bad thing?"

"A very good thing. I like the energy of New York, don't get me wrong. But there are people crammed on top of each other, covering nearly every inch. Here, even surrounded by people, it feels like...solitude. Contentment. In New York, everyone's climbing and reaching and trying to be more or better. Here, none of that matters. You just *are*."

He watched me, as if trying to solve a puzzle that was missing pieces. His probing expression only urged me on.

"Like in New York," I said, "I'm a small person in a big place. Here, I'm in a small place, so I feel bigger. Like I matter more here." The words sounded ridiculous even to my ears. I clamped my mouth shut, reminding myself that this man was my boss. He didn't need to know the inner workings of my mind.

He turned his gaze back to the road, where the occasional tiny supply truck or scooter rode by. "Once, you asked me why I chose this island. It's because here, thousands of miles from home, I found myself." He fixed a stare on me, watching carefully for my reaction.

I nodded, feeling the truth of it. "That's the perfect description. I see why you come here every chance you get. If I were you, I'd never leave."

"That's always a temptation. But I go to New York because some things are better done in person."

"Like firing money-stealing wedding planners," I said. *And finding replacements who almost get knocked out cold during a game they've played since age twelve.*

"Precisely. As much as I'd love to let the company go, it's keeping the island running right now. Too many people depend on that resort and its weddings for their livelihood."

I took him in, this rare vulnerability that he never showed anyone else, and felt honored to see it. "I hope the islanders know how much you love them."

He nodded. "They've given me far more than I could ever give them."

I drew myself taller. "There's only one thing your island is missing."

"Oh?"

"A library."

Surprise crossed his face, then disappeared into the Chase vault as quickly as it had come. "I've been working on that, actually. What kind of books do you recommend we stock it with?"

"Thrillers. Horror. And books about...fate."

"Fate," he repeated, as if trying to understand.

"You know, stories about how the universe is both intricate and simple. Stories that communicate the depth of the human experience. Not light and fluffy but deep and gritty and all-consuming, the kind you can't put down, and then when you finish, it's rendered you completely unable to do anything else because it stays with you. The kind of book that makes you feel you and the author were meant to connect in this way, and the story fills a hole in your soul that you didn't know existed."

Oh my gosh, Daphne. Bring it down a notch.

"And stories about sloths," I added. "Because they're cute."

He said nothing for a long while, and I mentally kicked myself for rambling on. If he hadn't made a library a priority already, the guy probably didn't even read. Why had I gone on and on about my love for books with a man who was only making conversation?

"I'll be on the lookout for a book like that," he said, motioning to the left. We stepped behind a building to a small square where a shed stood prominently in the middle, surrounded by carefully-placed barrels. A tiny restaurant, I realized, the size of a food truck with a smattering of cafe lights on top. A sign in the window read CASA DE MARIANELA.

I could barely read the sign at all because of the long line of people.

Chase was taking me to lunch? Or did he intend to pick up food for the rest of the staff? Although that much food would be hard to transport on a motorcycle.

"It has to be a thirty-minute wait," I pointed out, but he completely ignored me as he strode toward the window.

The woman on the other side spotted him, smiled, and called something behind her. By the time we reached the window, she had an entire tray of food ready. Not a bag for a bunch of people, but a tray for two. For us.

"*Mi favorita*," Chase said when he reached the window, making the woman grin. Then he leaned over and whispered something to her. She nodded, her smile widening, and wrote something down.

"*Gracias, Marianela*," he finally called, striding toward me with the tray in his hands.

She gave a little curtsy and replied in broken English. "Anything for you, Chase."

Of course—he had his own rules here. Chase got what he wanted, when he wanted it. Including lunch with his wedding planner and fake girlfriend, apparently.

My heart kicked up a notch.

He stopped at a barrel that apparently doubled as a table, and set the tray down. "I had them put the toppings on the side. I wasn't sure what you like."

The food already looked incredible. "Spice in whatever form I can get it."

He nodded approvingly. "No wonder you love the island. You already eat like a local."

It felt odd eating while standing, but somehow also appropriate. I loved how active everyone was here, full of color and spirit and everything that made life fun. Their food matched their lifestyle—peppered in layers of spicy depth that made my very veins sweat. I tried not to eat too quickly, which was hard considering the delicious food. A couple of times, I caught Chase watching me with that thoughtful look again.

Each time, I looked away. I couldn't let him find what he was searching for now.

When we'd both finished, I noticed our "table" was far from the others. The guy truly did like his solitude. "It seems like everyone knows you here. You didn't need to distance us on my account."

He paused. "That has nothing to do with you. Actually…it wasn't the food I wanted to show you. It was this table."

Confused, I looked it up and down. Identical to the others, as far as I could tell. "Why?"

"You asked me why the business means so much to me. The answer to that starts right here. This is where my uncle once told me something that would change my life. I'd be honored if you would allow me to share."

I felt a little touched. Something told me this wasn't a story he shared often. "Of course."

"You probably know about my parents." He looked to me for confirmation, and I nodded. "Suddenly I was a seven-year-old orphan whose world had just dropped from beneath his feet. You probably understand how that felt better than anyone."

"I don't remember much about my mom," I admitted, "but I do remember the fear of going to a new home, being told I had a new family."

Chase nodded. "I hope your experience was better than mine. From day one, my uncle made it clear he didn't want to be my caretaker. He provided shelter, a nanny, and an allowance. That was about it." He glanced my direction. "I don't mean for this to be depressing. It's just that you need the backstory for everything to make sense."

"You don't need to apologize. Please, share whatever you're comfortable with. I'm here for all of it."

"You are," he said softly. "Aren't you?"

"Truly."

A few more seconds passed that could have been years for all I knew. My heart pumped so loudly, I could swear he heard it.

He wore a strange look now, as if realizing something that surprised him. "Thank you."

In that moment, I felt an odd ache in my chest. Did this man not have anyone in his life that he could talk to openly? Even more importantly, why had he singled me out as someone he could trust?

That second question bothered me more than anything... because out of everyone he knew, I was the most likely to betray that trust.

He stared at his hands. "My uncle wanted me to go to NYU since campus wasn't far from where we lived, so I chose to travel to the furthest place away I could imagine. I recruited my friend Tanner to come with me and we moved here. Spent an entire summer learning Spanish and getting to know the people. I'd intended to go back by September, but by November I still hadn't come home, so my uncle decided to join me here for Thanksgiving." He chuckled bitterly. "I spent a fortune getting the food ready. Called in favors from friends, told the entire town. Everyone showed up to greet him when he arrived. We treated him like a king. Yet through the entire dinner, all he did was complain. Said he wanted to get some real food and left to go in search of some."

I gritted my teeth. How humiliating and disrespectful.

"I followed and caught up with him here at the taco stand.

He stood at this barrel, staring at a tray of tacos like he thought it would reach out and swallow him whole. I'm ashamed of how I acted now, but I still steamed from how he'd treated my friends. So I yelled at him. Called him selfish and spoiled and a few other words I won't repeat."

All understandable reactions, I wanted to say.

"He watched me with this sad look on his face. When I'd finished, he told me he hadn't come for Thanksgiving Dinner at all. He'd just been diagnosed with stage-four cancer and wanted to see what I'd made of myself in this world, to decide whether to make me his heir despite my lack of interest in his business dealings."

My head snapped up. "He was dying and yet still trying to decide what you meant to him? His only family?"

"Apparently. He meant far more to me than I ever did to him, it seems. Yet I felt horrified at the thought of losing him too. Deep down, I sensed that he was still mourning the loss of his sister and bonding with her son, with me, would be acknowledging that loss." He traced the top of the barrel absently with his finger. "It's taken me over a decade to realize why. When you love someone, you risk more than losing them. You risk losing the part of yourself that belongs to them."

An image immediately came to mind—of my Dad, sitting in his bed. Pale and groaning with that stupid ball cap covering his balding head. Mom, looking a little green and very tired. Both trying to shield me from the truth and cutting me out instead. In the end, that part had hurt the most—that they hadn't given me the option of suffering with them. That they hadn't acknowledged the fact that potentially losing Dad meant potentially losing some of myself too.

Chase saw my face and frowned. "Is something wrong?"

"No. It's just that I'm . . . remembering someone."

"Let's talk about something else, then."

"Not a chance," I said quickly. "I want to hear the rest."

He hesitated. "I didn't mean for this entire conversation to center around my childhood."

"You're ready to talk, and I—I'm not. But I can listen. There's nowhere else in the world I would rather be than with you, here, right now. Please continue."

He paused before seeing my sincerity. Finally he heaved a big sigh. "There isn't much more to tell. Standing right here, at this barrel, he said I was a disappointment and would never succeed on my own. When I told him my idea of success was different from his, he laughed. Eventually, though, I did fly back to New York with him. Took him to doctors' appointments, and even the office when he felt well enough. Called for at-home care when he didn't. I still wasn't interested in his work, and I think he knew that. But I *was* interested in serving him until the end. Not because I wanted his inheritance, but because it was the right thing to do. It's what my mom would have wanted." Chase scowled. "I didn't realize he'd put me in his will after all until six days after his death. When his attorney told me, I only felt disappointment."

I stared at him. "Why?"

"I'm not sure. Perhaps because I wanted nothing to do with his line of work, yet here I was, suddenly a major shareholder. He bought struggling companies at rock-bottom prices, turned them around, and sold them at a huge profit. He also bought land and buildings in estate sales or bankruptcy deals and flipped them for top dollar. He took advantage of those most in need, or at least that was how I chose to see it. I immediately sold his shares and decided to put the rest where it was most needed, but couldn't determine where that would be. I returned to this island to think it through in the one place I felt most at home, only to find a large real estate firm circling the smaller resort company like vultures. They wanted to seize the resort and build at least twelve more high-rise buildings. The new Cancun, they kept saying."

"So you swooped in and saved the island in its natural state."

He nodded. "I've been to Cancun. It's beautiful, but some tourists seem so entitled. Those ones care little for those who already live there or the generations to come. That was the last thing I wanted for the island that helped me find myself."

It all made sense. "But what about the events company?"

Chase sighed. "If it weren't for the revenue for the islanders, I would sell it in a second. The whole operation has done worse and worse every year. Last summer we went from bleak to dire. The board gave me one last summer to show this can still work. I thought these two high-revenue weddings might do it, but with only one going through...it'll be close. Very close."

Gulp. "I see. And if you have to sell?"

His jaw clenched. "I've already donated the island to its own people and I won't take it back. The events company can be sold, but I'll owe a substantial amount of money on our contracts and the building. The accountants say I'll never recover financially if that happens."

I wasn't sure I wanted to know, but I had to ask. "And the resort?"

Chase leveled his gaze at me. "The real estate firm bent on turning the entire island into New Cancun? They've staked their claim, and now they're waiting me out. The owner, in particular, dislikes me and can't wait to destroy everything I've built." He exhaled deeply. "That man is Veronica's dad."

EIGHTEEN

WE SPENT the rest of the afternoon together, walking around town and discussing his favorite memories of the island. He didn't want to discuss Veronica and her father, but at least I'd managed to pry from him the fact that Veronica's father hadn't approved of her dating Chase in the first place.

The whole thing sounded like one huge mess. And I'd thought my relationship with Ty was complicated.

All too soon, Chase dropped me off near my bungalow, and I closed the door behind me, leaning against it like a swooning TV heroine.

Wow.

It was the only word I could think of to describe the day. First the volleyball incident, which seemed like a blur, followed by the very real and poignant experience of Chase carrying me to the resort medical center. Then the trip to town, which I recalled in sharp detail, our taco lunch, and his uncle story. So intimate. So...just the two of us.

I'd been given a glimpse into Chase that nobody else got to see, and that kind of trust felt both incredible and awful at the same time. Why had I been so free with him today, as if we were friends? We were *not* friends. We couldn't be friends, not when I planned to interfere with the wedding that had become his last hope.

I knew exactly how betrayal felt, yet I planned to betray Chase. Between my mom's behavior the day of my dad's surgery and the night Ty had dumped me, I understood that gut-wrenching, heart-slicing feeling of being hurt by someone I trusted. Could I do that to Chase when he'd entrusted me with everything that mattered to him? Especially when he had so few people in his life right now?

I tried to see the world from his perspective. Dead parents. Dead uncle who'd left him more money than he knew what to do with. Only one thing that meant anything to him and that would fail the moment I stole Ty away.

When I entered my room, I halted in my tracks. A box wrapped in brown paper and tied with a sophisticated black ribbon sat on my bed.

I jumped onto the mattress, folded my legs under me, and hefted the box into my lap with a grunt. Heavy. Beneath the bow sat an envelope. I tore it open and held my breath as I read the words in neat handwriting.

Daphne,

Here are some of my favorites. I don't know if these communicate the depth of the human experience, but they did serve to fill some of the admittedly many holes in my soul. I look forward to discussing them with you.

Yours,
Chase

Not Mr. Everett. Not Ms. Porter.

Daphne and Chase.

Reverently, I stroked the package, afraid of what I would find inside. Finally, I tore the box open. It contained eight new books, all hardcovers—several thrillers, one horror novel, an epic fantasy, a book about sloths, and to my surprise, a couple of romances. Each had a PURA VIDA BOOKSTORE label on the back.

When had he done this? I'd been with him all afternoon. Did it have something to do with his whispered conversation with Marianela at the restaurant?

Regardless, I couldn't get over how good his name and mine looked together on the same card. It made a little shiver wriggle up and down my spine.

I whipped out my phone and shot him a quick text.

Thank you for the books. I'll start the first one tonight.

The little dots danced about, signaling that he was typing. A second later, his reply appeared.

I'm glad you like them. Which will you read first?

I grinned as I answered and hit Send. *Not the romances, I'm afraid.*

A pause, then his reply. *I missed the mark on those, huh?*

Not in the least. It's just that this beautiful island has replaced all my hopes and dreams. Those poor shirtless heroes would never be able to compete.

I felt his laugh across the distance that separated us more than heard it. His reply took a moment to show up. *Good thing they're fictional, or they'd be devastated at what they're missing.*

My breath hitched.

I stared at the words. They didn't disappear, no matter how many times I read them.

There was nothing fake about that flirtatious line with this conversation taking place in the privacy of our own homes and hidden on our phones. Nobody else would see it. So why had he said it?

And how was I supposed to respond? *Thank you?* He'd given a compliment, but that wasn't the type of compliment a boss gave to his employee. That wasn't even a compliment one friend gave to another. In a single text, Chase had launched us over a line that I didn't want to acknowledge existed.

Mom always said that humor and changing the subject cured all awkwardness. Time to try out that advice now.

Speaking of competing, I texted, *I want a rematch on the court one of these days. My pride won't take no for an answer.*

He wrote back immediately. *As much as I'd love to finish the job, I have a better idea. Meet me at the boardwalk nature tour tomorrow after work. There's something else I want to show you.*

A little thrill seized my chest at the thought of seeing Chase again before I stomped it down and mentally burned it. Ty and Veronica were scheduled for the nature tour at the boardwalk tomorrow evening. That meant Chase only wanted us to be seen there together as a couple. How many times would I have to remind myself of that?

Of course, I wrote back. *Looking forward to it.*

That, at least, was the truth.

NINETEEN

When I arrived at the boardwalk, I positively squealed. "It's a sloth tour?"

Chase, who leaned against the ticket shed, chuckled. "It's called the rainforest nature tour, but yes, sloths are a perk."

I'd only ever seen sloths from behind glass. I practically bounced on the wooden planks beneath my feet. "Will we see one?"

He shaded his eyes with his free hand and looked up at the sun. "It might be a little bright for them today, but possibly. I know a few spots they like to hang out."

I'd never been more tempted to kiss Chase Everett. Of course, that was against the rules. The rules that I'd set myself and we both agreed on and would definitely *not* be breaking today. So instead, I slid my arms under his and gave him a hug. "Thank you."

"It's nothing." His voice sounded oddly rough.

Our tour guide, a trim woman sporting a boyish haircut and brown uniform with a heavy utility belt, arrived five minutes later and immediately took charge. I worried about hearing her with a group this large, but she had a loud, gritty voice.

"Let's go, everyone," she called and marched down the boardwalk at a breakneck pace.

I moved to follow, but Chase's hand gripped mine and he leaned in close, sending delightful tingles down my skin. "Let everyone else go first."

How did the man smell so good this late in the day?

The group shuffled along, chattering excitedly to one another. A young boy gave the boardwalk a few test jumps as he held his father's hand. "Are we going to see tigers, Daddy?"

The father laughed. "I certainly hope not. Maybe crocodiles though."

"Will they eat us?"

"Not if we stay on the boardwalk."

I expected to see fear on the boy's face at that, but his grin only widened. Then the group behind them cut them off from view.

"We don't see enough kids here," Chase murmured. "They're far more fun than the parents."

I elbowed him in the side. "You *are* a softie. I knew it."

He only grunted.

"A sloth tour?" a familiar voice snapped. "What am I, six?"

I turned to see Ty and Veronica step onto the boardwalk. She wore a swimsuit beneath a cover-up too sheer to deserve the word and a wide, floppy hat shading her thick sunglasses.

Ty's face was burgundy as he faced her down. "You said you wanted to explore the island."

"The beach, Ty," she moaned. "I wanted to explore the beach, not some rainforest full of mosquitos and snakes. Besides, we don't have time for this. Don't you realize how much there is to do in the next few days?"

I'd forgotten—today was Wednesday and the wedding

would take place this weekend. A clump of nerves sat at the pit of my stomach. I had to get Ty alone somehow, to see how he really felt before it was too late. That wasn't likely to happen today, though. With Chase using me to avoid Veronica and the simple fact that Veronica would be everywhere Ty was, I hadn't exactly thought this whole fake dating thing through.

Ty finally saw us staring at him and cleared his throat. "Hey, guys."

Veronica's eyes found Chase. In less than a second, her entire countenance changed from dark to light. Her voice practically jumped an octave. "Chase. Fancy meeting you here."

Chase stiffened. "You too, Veronica. I thought you didn't like animals."

The tone of his voice, tight and a bit too strained, pulled my gaze to him. He stared at Ty and Veronica with an expression that I couldn't read behind his dark sunglasses. Unfortunate, because I *really* wanted to know what he was thinking right now. What did this man see when he looked at Veronica? A dodged bullet, or the one who got away?

A new thought practically took my breath away. Could Chase be having the same thoughts about Veronica that I was having about Ty?

"Daphne, on the other hand," Chase said, pulling me closer and making me realize I'd stepped away, "is looking forward to this, and I won't allow her to miss it. If you could excuse us." He slid his fingers down my arm, found my palm, and cupped my hand in his as if it had been designed to hold mine. I felt the trail of his fingers like a volcanic river running down my arm.

Sometimes Chase made it really hard to focus.

"Go back to the hotel, then," Ty muttered to Veronica. "I'm not missing this either."

I spared a quick glance backward in time to catch two very important things.

First, Ty had begun to follow us. He glowered at our backs, although his altercation with his fiancée explained that.

Second, Veronica stared after him, her face full of suspicion. Ty hadn't tried very hard to convince her to come along, especially for a man who would be marrying her in a matter of days.

For a moment, the only sound was our feet on the boardwalk and the chirping of birds around us.

At the last second, Veronica groaned. "Fine! Let's get it over with."

And our not-so-pleasant foursome began.

❤ ❤ ❤ ❤ ❤

I saw not one, but three sloths.

Chase pointed them out long before the tour guide did. Then he brought me around to the best place to see them, beneath a tree canopy further down. I took at least thirty photos of the cute little guys while Chase watched me, a half smile on his face.

A moment later, the tour guide called Chase over for a quick discussion of who-knew-what. Considering Veronica was in the group, smiling sweetly at him, I could only imagine that she'd found some excuse to get the tour guide to bring him over.

As his official fake girlfriend, I should have gone over to rescue him. But at that moment, Ty appeared at my side.

No amount of humor or subject-changing could improve what surely qualified as the Book of World Records' most awkward silence in the history of time. Ty and I stood a few feet apart, avoiding each other's gazes and pretending to be interested in the rainforest around us.

"So he's treating you well?" Ty asked, his voice a full octave too high.

I grinned. "Very well."

"Good."

His voice carried a false note, which finally compelled me to look at him. "What?"

"Nothing."

"Don't nothing me. What do you mean?"

Ty glanced at Chase, still chatting with the tour guide behind us. "It's just that...I've heard things."

The pool guy came back to mind. I hadn't seen him in a few days. "You'll need to be more specific."

Ty leaned in closer, still eyeing Chase. "Just rumors."

"Like?"

"Like he burned through his fortune too quickly, and his employees are going to take the hit for it."

I thought about what he'd said yesterday about the company. "Well, islands and million-dollar corporations aren't cheap. But he's changing lives on this island."

Ty cocked his head in that way I knew so well. It screamed *You're not telling the full story.*

"He's a really good man, Ty. I know it's hard for people to see, but once you get to know him—" I stopped. Did I even really know him? Why did I feel it necessary to defend Chase when I'd come all this way to win Ty? I should be telling sob stories right now so he'd feel sorry for me and try to pull off some kind of rescue. At the very least, we should be discussing Veronica right now. Who knew when we'd get another opportunity like this?

But I couldn't throw Chase under the bus, not even now. Not when the accusations were flat-out wrong.

"Chase is a really good actor," Ty continued. He seemed completely oblivious to the fact that his wife-to-be was currently flirting with Chase, both surrounded by a crowd of tourists. "He doesn't let people near him because he has so much to hide. If he's letting you in, you have to ask yourself why. I guarantee there's a reason. There's always a reason with him."

"You're one to talk," I snapped. "You broke up with me because I had no money, and then you get engaged to Veronica freaking Loyal? Really?"

Ty's mouth pressed together in disapproval. "All I'm saying is that I'm sorry I hurt you. It was wrong of me to treat you that way. I don't want to watch that hurt play out all over again with a self-absorbed billionaire who's never had a relationship last more than two months."

"You don't get to worry about someone you dumped," I said, my voice low and dangerous. "You don't get to swoop in here and act like you care, because you don't. If you did, you wouldn't be marrying that woman." I stomped past him. If the group wanted to take ten years to get past a single tree, I'd leave without them.

Ty grabbed my arm. "I do care," he hissed. "You don't date someone for two years and suddenly stop loving them in a day."

I shook my arm free, gaping at him. "What are you saying?"

"I'm saying..." His eyes pleaded for me to understand without voicing the words. "I'm saying I don't know. It's complicated."

He'd dodged the words I needed him to say.

"I *am* happy," Ty said, his tone anything but happy.

Chase appeared behind Ty, a stormy expression on his face. He'd obviously seen Ty grab my arm and wanted to show him a thing or two. But with Ty being a client, he'd have to show his claim on me in a dignified yet decisive way.

Curse the no kissing thing.

Curse it to Hades.

Chase must have been thinking the same thing, because his gaze met mine, his eyebrows lifted in a question that I read clear as day--a question that I answered with a quick nod before I could think through the consequences.

For the cause, I told myself.

Chase crossed the distance between us in two strides, practically shoving Ty out of the way. Before I knew what was happening, he swept me into his arms, twirled, dipped me so deeply I rose onto my toes, and claimed my mouth. Like, took possession of it in a way I didn't know was possible. His lips moved on mine as if we were alone, not surrounded by clients in the middle of a jungle boardwalk. I found myself melting into his arms, utterly and completely at his mercy.

And then I was back on my feet, swaying like a drunk person and trying to refocus my blurry eyes on a stunned Ty.

"Hey there," Chase said to Ty, as if barely noticing he was there. "All good?"

Ty's face had turned bright purple. "Uh. Y—yeah. Everything's...fine."

"Good. It almost looked like you two were arguing. But appearances can be deceiving, can't they?" Even behind his glasses, I saw intensity in Chase's eyes. His tone had dropped in warning with those last few words. The implications there almost made me shiver.

Ty nodded vigorously. "Absolutely. Of course. Nothing but an honest disagreement. I'd better find Veronica. Don't want to miss those, um, butterflies."

"Sloths," I corrected softly, but he'd already fled and I barely cared. Chase filled my vision and it felt nearly impossible to remember at the moment that Ty even existed somewhere. "What was *that*?"

"A message," he said, his voice hard. "What did he say to you?"

The man had just kissed me like I'd never been kissed before in my entire life, and he wanted to know about our conversation? I reminded myself that the kiss meant nothing, that his "message" was simply an attempt to thwart any ideas on his part, but I'd expected a simple peck on the lips. That would have done just fine. Why had Chase chosen to kiss me thoroughly enough to make my legs shaky for the next week?

"Nothing of consequence," I finally managed. "Just a very old argument that doesn't matter anymore." I released Chase's hand and folded my arms, starting after the rest of the group.

"Don't," Chase said behind me, a faint growl in his voice. A second later, he slipped in front of me, blocking my path.

I looked up at him. "Don't what?"

He gestured to my stance. "This. Don't let him or anyone else make you stand like that. Not ever."

I saw myself through his eyes—arms folded, shoulders hunched, probably a hurt expression. Not for the reasons Chase believed though.

Ty was wrong. Chase wasn't the lying, manipulating one. I was.

Forcing myself to straighten, I met Chase's firm gaze. "I'm fine. It's just the memories, that's all."

A flash of pain appeared in his eyes. Faster than a bolt of lightning, it was gone, making me wonder if it had ever been there at all.

"He hurt you," Chase said, his expression darkening.

I couldn't answer that truthfully, yet I couldn't think of a single lie to dissuade this man who suddenly seemed intent on exploring every crevice of my heart and soul.

"It doesn't matter. You came over at the perfect time." I brought my fingers to my mouth, remembering. As I did, his eyes followed and rested on my lips.

Why did I want to wrap my hands around his head, pull

him down, and continue what he'd just started? How could I have said yes to something so foolish as a kiss?

How could I possibly be happy with Ty or any other man after being kissed by Chase Everett?

"Um," I said, tearing myself away and starting to walk. "The group is moving again. Maybe we'll see another sloth family."

Chase caught up in two massive strides. "Heaven forbid I keep you from your furry rodent friends."

I stuck a finger into the sky for emphasis. "*Not* rodents."

"Probably not, but they look like it. And that smile? It's a sinister one, I'm sure of it. Look at them the wrong way, and they'll murder you in your sleep."

"Thankfully, it'll take them about three years to reach my bungalow," I pointed out. "I'll be long gone by then."

The reminder dampened the moment like a raincloud over a patch of sunshine. Even if Ty did marry Veronica, the dry summer wedding season would end in a matter of weeks. I would face New York and a sterile office building, and Chase would stay behind.

Our fake dating agreement had an even shorter shelf life. The moment Ty and Veronica got married, I would lose both Chase *and* Ty.

"Any other animals you adore?" Chase asked as we walked, hand in hand. It was beginning to feel comfortable now. "We don't have a zoo on the island, but I'll see what I can do."

"Horses." My answer came immediately. "I haven't ridden since I left Rosie at home. My gray mare."

Chase gave my hand a squeeze. "Preparations for the next rehearsal dinner don't begin until noon tomorrow. That's enough time for a short trail ride together in the morning if you're game. Say, around eight?"

As sweet as the offer was, it came from the wrong mouth. I couldn't invest in a fake relationship with Chase with my future at stake. I'd come so far and made so many plans, yet Ty couldn't even express his feelings so our relationship could get where we needed it to be.

And now that kiss...well, I had some serious work to do if I didn't want him to run back into Veronica's arms.

"Nobody would see us together on a trail ride, Chase," I reminded him.

He frowned a bit, so I plunged on.

"It sounds like fun, don't get me wrong. It's just that the books and the horses and all that—I don't get the point when everything will be back to normal in a few days."

He gave me a long look from behind his dark sunglasses. I couldn't quite read the expression there, but I could sense his disapproval. I'd definitely said something to offend him, or at the very least, hurt him a little.

I was about to apologize when he released my hand. Not meeting my gaze, he said, "I forgot to tell the tour guide something. I'll see you at the end."

Then he walked away.

TWENTY

THE NEXT MORNING, I went to the stables at eight, hoping to get the chance to apologize. When Chase didn't show, I saddled an old Appaloosa gelding named Tennyson and rode him around the corral for a few minutes before finally giving up. My heart simply wasn't in it today. Riding made me miss home and Rosie more than ever. I longed for the familiarity of my loft bed.

I longed for Chase.

Our agreement didn't end until Ty's wedding in three days, yet I'd managed to insult him and drive away any last moments we could have enjoyed together. The fact that it had probably been for the best didn't help.

I went the office only to find my mind wandering, refusing to focus on work. After twenty minutes of trying, I grabbed the Magic 8 ball again and shook it as hard as I could without launching it across the room.

"Am I pursuing the wrong guy?" I snapped, and turned it over to watch the window.

The words appeared immediately. *My sources say no.*

I groaned and tossed it back into its drawer before pulling up my horoscope app, determined to get at least a hint of something that resonated with my heart.

"In times of doubt, you must cling to what you know is right," the little bubble said. "Don't let outside forces distract you from your goal."

I wanted to punch something at this point. Clearly I wasn't in the right headspace to be cross-checking bride champagne choices against inventory lists, so I left the office and headed back to my cozy bungalow.

With three hours left until I needed to arrive at the kitchen, I grabbed the remote and turned to the most reliable source of comfort in my life—Cavil McNeil. A few clicks and I let myself relax into the sofa. It had been weeks since I'd seen my favorite movie, which meant I was long overdue for another movie binge. It wouldn't quite be the same without Bridget here, but hey. Where else to watch an old black-and-white western than three hundred yards away from a beautiful beach?

I lost myself in the man of my dreams, the tough-guy essence of him and his partially shaved chin and razor-sliced jawline. His deep bass voice filled my living room and my chest and my very soul. The best part? The way he looked at Samantha when she walked into the tavern—as if he'd just found the woman who made his life complete. And they hadn't even spoken a word to each other.

Yet minutes later, they kissed behind the saloon because the romantic tension was so intense that everyone in the entire bar felt it.

Chase was as close to Cavill as any man I'd ever met, but not in any way that mattered. Not for me. They just didn't make men like that anymore. They didn't make *romances* like that anymore. Such charisma. Such...I don't know, knowing what they wanted. And to be on the receiving end of a kiss like that? So real. So meaningful. Not a simple message, but an entire novel written only for her. Samantha didn't understand how good she—

A knock sounded at the door.

I sat bolt upright. Only two people knew I lived here, and I doubted Agwe would have come by when he could just as easily text. That left only one possibility.

"Just a minute," I called, sweeping the coffee table trash into my hand and shoving it into my pockets. Throwing a dark glance at the messy kitchen, I hurried to the door and yanked it open.

Chase stood there...in faded jeans and a button-up shirt with the sleeves rolled halfway to his elbow.

He looked *good*.

Like, Cavil McNeil good. But without the hat shading his eyes. Or the cowboy boots.

Chase cleared his throat, and I realized I'd just been looking him up and down for a good five seconds.

"Hi," I said, fixing my gaze firmly on his. *There you go, Daphne. Eyes on the prize...er, eyes.* I definitely meant eyes. "Did you need something?"

He glanced past me to the TV, which I hadn't bothered to pause, just as Cavil McNeil told the woman of his dreams that his life wouldn't be complete without her.

"Oh, Cavil," she moaned from behind me. "I knew you were the one."

"Doesn't sound like any chick flick I've seen," Chase said.

"Just an old cowboy show." I shrugged. "Riding Tennyson this morning got me in the mood."

"I'm glad you did take him out. The old guy needs more exercise than he gets." His gaze dropped to his feet, which shifted beneath him.

"I was hoping you'd be there," I hinted. "I wanted to apologize for what I said yesterday. It was thoughtless of me."

He waved it off without meeting my eyes. "No need."

This felt so weird. Chase Everett, on my doorstep, looking uncomfortable?

"Um, do you want to come in?" I asked, stepping back and pulling the door open wider.

"Sure." His frame filled the doorway, and then we stood just inches apart in the tiny entryway.

"I'll get the door," I said just as he said, "Let me get that for you." His hand grasped mine in an attempt to grip the door and instantly recoiled as if he'd touched something hot.

"Sorry," he murmured, letting me swing the door closed the rest of the way.

We stared at each other.

He said nothing, simply looked around in discomfort.

My stomach churning, I pointed toward the couch I'd been sprawled across a moment ago. "Do you want to sit down?"

Without a word, he strode toward the sofa, grabbed the pillows off one of the cushions, sat, and dumped the armful of pillows on the ground.

I stared at the discarded pillows.

"Oh, did you need those?" he asked, plucking them off the ground and shoving them back onto the couch next to him.

Men. "No, they're for decoration. And you just covered them in dust. And then spread that dust to the sofa."

He flipped over a cream pillow, wiped it clean, and placed it neatly back onto the couch. "I'll never understand why women like these things."

"They make the sofa feel more welcoming. You know, cradle your body as you're sitting? Make you feel like you're in bed, watching TV?"

I cringed inwardly at the fact that I'd used the words

"cradle your body" and "bed" in the same sentence in a conversation with Chase Everett, but he didn't seem to think anything of it.

"Why not put a TV in front of your bed then?" he mused. "I'm sure Agwe could install it for you."

"No," I said quickly, moving the pillows aside so I could sit next to him. "I like this setup. If I had to sit in bed to watch TV, I'd fall asleep."

He stared at me, unblinking. "So you...bring the bed to you."

"Exactly." I paused. "I mean, no, not really. It's just that— Chase, I really am sorry about yesterday. I didn't mean to minimize the nice things you've done. You don't need a reason to be kind, and I shouldn't have suggested otherwise."

He leaned forward and pressed his fingertips together, staring at the wall. "Actually, I came to apologize for my own behavior. I made you uncomfortable yesterday. Sometimes I assume things, and I'm not great at reading people. I wanted you to know that with what time remains of our little bargain, we'll follow your lead."

You assumed what, exactly? I hardly dared breathe, despite desperately wanting to know what he meant and also being terrified of the answer.

Chase must have seen the question on my face, because his expression immediately closed as he gestured to the TV. "You like cowboy shows?"

I let myself exhale, grateful for the change of subject. "Not just any show. *The Cowboy's Last Chase.* This is Cavil McNeil's greatest work. He's a legend."

Chase stared at me as if seeing me in a new light. "You can access almost any show from around the world, yet you're watching a movie made a hundred years ago?"

"Eighty years, and you don't understand. The scene when

his love rides away on the train, and he rides to stop her? Drops everything, including the criminals, and gallops off with his trusty steed to claim the future he knows they can still have? Tom Cruise only wishes he could pull that off. Best stunts, best music, best scene ever."

"Really." He looked thoughtful. "I'd like to decide that for myself, if you wouldn't mind the company."

In that instant, I remembered the time I'd asked Ty to watch this show with me. I'd even made pizza for the occasion. He'd spent half the movie grumbling and the other half texting. At the train scene, he'd actually made fun of my cowboy, ridiculing him for chasing after his love and taunting Cavil as he tried desperately to win her back.

Did I really want a replay of that experience with Chase? Could I hand him something I loved and watch him rip it to shreds?

"You have to see the whole thing from the beginning," I warned him. "You won't get it unless you see how their relationship started. It's one of the best meet cutes ever."

I waited, expecting him to tease me for the term or run at the first hint of a chick flick.

"Fine." He slapped his thighs and rose to his feet.

Wait. What?

Chase saw my confusion and smirked. "If you're starting the movie over, I'm making popcorn."

"I don't have any," I said, feeling bewildered.

"Yes, you do. I put it in the far-right bottom drawer just before you arrived. Filled the fridge too. Can't be accused of starving my employees after that long flight."

I tried to picture Chase hurrying to my quarters from a long flight that had arrived only slightly earlier than mine, tidying everything in preparation for my arrival. This definitely wasn't the boss I'd seen at the office in New York. "I figured you sent Agwe to do everything."

"He offered, but I insisted. I read in your employee file that you'd never been on an island before, so I thought I'd make this as homey as possible. For the record, the pillows were *not* my idea." He grimaced and went into the kitchen.

I chuckled, grabbing the remote and restarting the movie just as I remembered the current state of my kitchen. Why hadn't I done the dishes this morning? Thankfully, I heard no complaints from Chase—only the sound of drawers and cupboards opening and closing.

Then I realized I'd be sitting next to Chase Everett and eating popcorn, and whipped out my cell phone to check my appearance.

Yikes. My post-horseback-riding hair looked windblown and wild, and my black bra strap peeked on one side of my wide shirt. I straightened everything, combed my hair back with my fingers, and pulled a few strands to frame my face before remembering it didn't matter whether Chase found me attractive.

Except he'd said he was bad at reading people. What exactly had he misread? If I had led him on somehow and then snapped at him for acting on that...no wonder the poor guy had been confused.

But if he'd acted on it because he wanted to, because he enjoyed my company...because he *liked* me...

The thought of this turning into anything more than a sham felt more surreal than a Salvador Dali painting. Chase dated millionaires—beach-wave women who got manicures, boob jobs, Botox, and instant social media followers. Not frumpy farm girl employees who chased grooms that didn't want them and watched ancient cowboy romances because fictional men could never break her heart.

The microwave beeped as the entire bungalow smelled like delicious melted butter...and shortly afterward, something not so delicious and very much burned. Chase cursed.

"That microwave runs hot," I warned. "You'll have to stop it early."

"Yeah. Figured that out."

Five minutes later, Chase returned with a giant bowl of popcorn (batch number two) and a couple of cups. He immediately settled onto the loveseat next to me, his leg resting against mine and sending pleasant zings ripping up and down my limbs.

He scooped a cup of popcorn, handed it to me, and gestured to the TV. "I'm ready to be wowed."

I hit Play on the remote and settled back. "I'm not sure you've been adequately prepared for the majesty of this moment, but I'll give you a chance."

"One chance is all I need." He filled his cup and dumped half of it into his mouth at once. It was all I could do not to stare. Here, in this moment, Chase seemed almost normal.

This felt normal. That was, perhaps, the most stunning revelation of all.

The movie passed quickly, yet seemed to take forever at the same time. Chase seemed completely engrossed, laughing at the funny parts and looking somber at the sad ones. When Samantha climbed onto the train and said goodbye, Chase shook his head in disappointment. All the right reactions, yet I felt hyper-focused on his every movement.

It shouldn't have mattered to me what he thought of my favorite movie.

But it did.

This moment felt incredibly significant, and I couldn't even pinpoint why.

When my hero and his horse jumped over the fallen tree to

reach the train, enabling him to leap onto the caboose and hunt his sweetheart down, I felt the same thrill I always did. Being loved like that—the idea of being so incredibly cherished that someone would risk their life to get you back—always made me a little emotional.

Chase leaned forward in his seat now, what remained of the popcorn completely forgotten on the coffee table, his eyes riveted to the screen.

"Wow," he said softly. "That wasn't even a stunt double."

"They got that all in one take," I told him.

"What are you doing here?" the heroine on the screen demanded, looking pouty on the screen as she rose from her seat on the train. "I thought I told you goodbye."

"Maybe so," the hero said, sweeping her into his arms. "But I never said it back. I'm not saying goodbye to you. Not now, not ever. Now, I won't say you're mine, because that's up to you. But darlin', I am utterly and completely yours."

The couple stared deeply into each others' eyes for a long moment as the music swelled. Then they both, together, leaned forward for a kiss more passionate than considered acceptable for the time. I'd analyzed this scene hundreds of times, and I still couldn't decide who leaned in first. They moved as one, a mirror image, two hearts becoming one with a single, definitive kiss that would change the course of their lives and bind their futures together.

I don't know how long I stared at the screen, feeling that moment change me as it always did, but when I looked back at Chase, I could tell he'd been watching me for some time. His expression was blank, completely and infuriatingly unreadable. But he couldn't hide the emotion in his eyes. There, in their dark depths, I saw my own feelings reflected back at me. A different kind of mirror altogether. Not black-and-white on a screen between two actors, but something more real. Something that actually existed.

Something I'd sensed in his kiss...that was most definitely *not* fake.

A terrified thrill swept through me now, like the nervous anticipation of boarding a roller coaster. Only this one wouldn't end thirty seconds from now. I felt my future diverge into two paths—the one I'd always expected and a second that felt new and bright and full of potential.

Slowly, his eyes flicked to my lips. He leaned closer, millimeter by agonizing millimeter. I saw the narrow scar hashing across one dark eyebrow, the slight crookedness of his nose on the right side. How his lips quirked upward and exposed a hidden dimple. The cleft in his chin that reminded me of a certain cowboy hero.

Chase Everett definitely qualified as a "distraction from my goal," or whatever the horoscope had said. But destiny hadn't met Chase Everett, or it would have shut its annoying little mouth.

As Chase's face hovered just above mine, I felt his breath on my lips. At some point, I'd tilted my face upward and slightly to the side. Even if my brain panicked, my body knew exactly what to do--except this time, nobody was watching. His breath, despite the buttered popcorn we'd both devoured, held a hint of peppermint.

He started to close the distance—and then stopped.

I found myself holding my breath, my chest screaming for air, and my heart hammering in my rib cage, trying desperately to escape.

This had to be some kind of medieval torture, waiting like this. Maybe he expected me to go in for the kill myself. Some kind of chivalry thing.

I leaned forward.

He leaned forward—

—and turned his head to swipe a handful of popcorn from the bowl.

"No kissing," he said with a wink, and shoved the kernels into his mouth.

Had he really just...?

Oh, it's on.

I grabbed the popcorn bowl and plunged my hands into it, grabbing the biggest handful I could before launching the kernels at him. He rolled behind the couch just in time. The popcorn sprayed the room like fluffy machine gun fire.

Chase swiped a handful off the floor and tossed it in my direction. I used the side of the bowl to protect my face and hair before jumping onto the couch and dumping the rest of the bowl over his head—or at least, where it had just been. Chase was on his feet again, holding both our half-full cups and smirking.

I dove behind the coffee table just as the popcorn pelted the wood and glass.

Moments later, we both collapsed onto the loveseat, laughing. I hadn't had this much fun in a long time. His laughter stopped long before mine did, though he still wore a smile as he watched me, examining every inch of my face. I almost wondered if he would move in again, for real this time.

"I saw your employee record," he finally said. "You grew up in the Midwest. Does that movie remind you of home?"

"My farm? A little."

"Do you miss it?"

"Every day."

He nodded, not seeming surprised. "New York is pretty far away. When was the last time you visited home?"

I exhaled, suddenly feeling vulnerable and not loving it.

"It's been a long time, and it will be a long while yet. My parents and I don't exactly see eye-to-eye."

He didn't press the issue. Instead, he said, "Which do you like better, New York or the farm?"

I cocked my head, considering his question. A year ago, I would have said New York without hesitation. But there was something about this island that made me miss home.

"There's a tall tree on the south end of our farm," I told him. "I hate letting my fear of heights control me, so as a teenager, I'd ride Rosie out there and let her graze while I challenged myself to see how high I could climb. On my eighteenth birthday, I finally made it to the top. We didn't have any tall buildings out there, obviously, and it's completely flat. So I'd never seen that view before. I still remember how it felt to see everything from above for the first time."

He studied my face. "Then you moved to New York, where looking down on the streets from the fortieth floor is commonplace."

"A little easier than climbing a two-hundred-year-old tree, I'll admit."

"Not quite the same, though, is it?"

The expression on his face made me shift in my chair. Being seen like this, examined and questioned, made me want to sprint toward the beach and hide in the waves. "No, it's not. Even now, I'd choose that tree over the Empire State Building any day."

He stood and offered a hand to help me up. My hand reached up of its own accord. He grasped it, yanked me clean off the couch, and gently pried the remote from my other hand to turn off the TV. Then, still holding my hand, he leaned over to whisper softly in my ear. "I have a favorite tree too, here on the island. I'd love to show it to you sometime if you'll allow me."

His breath against my ear sent all kinds of weird sensations through my body. Ty had touched me yesterday and whispered like this. Had I felt anything at all? I couldn't even remember.

I checked my watch. "We have thirty minutes before I need to start helping in the kitchens. Is that enough time?"

It was the right answer. Chase looked pleased. "If it isn't, I'll have Agwe take your place for a bit. I don't think anyone will miss us."

TWENTY-ONE

RIDING in Chase's sporty black car, we took the main street for a few miles and then pulled onto a winding road behind a few older buildings and a farm, gradually easing downward until we reached the thick of the rainforest. He parked in a gravel area that barely looked habitable and led me to the beginning of a path scarcely wide enough for two people. Chase stepped onto it confidently, as if he'd been here a hundred times. He probably had.

I put my focus into trying not to trip on the occasional tree root or loose stone. The last thing I needed was another trip to the doctor.

After a few minutes, I noticed the rainforest around us looking darker than before with the exception of bright patterns on the forest floor from the sun. The patchwork of light and shadow almost felt like art—a painting that only adventurers and wildlife got to enjoy.

Soon the darkness lifted and the light returned. Ahead, the sky looked bright and welcoming, but also a little...pinkish?

"Pink Sand Beach," Chase said. "My favorite tree overlooks it."

I gasped. "There's a pink sand beach too? This is the coolest island ever."

Chase smiled while I hurried on ahead, eager to see what he was talking about. The sand did indeed have a pinkish hue to it. Or rather, it was the tiny pink shells glittering in the sand. I knelt to scoop up a handful and examined it from different angles.

"Beautiful," I told him.

"I agree."

Chase leaned against a monstrous palm tree that seemed larger than the rest, his arms folded as he watched me. The position made his biceps fill his shirt sleeves in a way that begged to be touched. My heart flipped just a bit.

I dumped the sand, stood, and walked over to him. We faced each other now, just like at the dance the other night. Only this time, the music that surrounded us was the scattered song of birds and the calls of an animal I couldn't identify. Chase's eyes, for once uncovered by his sunglasses and vulnerable, searched mine. For what, I couldn't begin to imagine.

I began listing off the reasons I shouldn't care for this man. First, he was my boss and I his employee. The list should have ended there, but even worse than that, I meant to betray him and steal someone else's groom. I'd come here to rob the man I now stood here gaping at. So why did it feel like none of that mattered anymore?

"I know you're tempted," Chase said, "but I have to tell you no."

I blinked. What was that supposed to mean?

His stern expression softened into a grin, and his hands slid around my waist. He pulled me closer and looked down at me. "You can't climb the tree," he whispered.

I rolled my eyes at the joke, but inside, my heart sprinted like a horse at the Kentucky Derby. This kind of thing happened in movies, not real life. Shouldn't he be holding some blonde bombshell on a yacht with the wind blowing through her hair and a smirk, not a coworker with buttery popcorn breath and a still-bruised nose?

"I thought I was calling the shots now," I told him, placing my hands on his chest and sliding them upward and around his hardened shoulders into an embrace. We'd danced in this exact position a few nights before, but for some reason, this time felt a zillion times more intimate.

Relief appeared in his expression at the gesture, and perhaps something more. Victory? He really hadn't known whether I would reciprocate. The billionaire worried about what I would do, what I would say.

Zodiac, I need to have some words with you, I wanted to scream into the universe. Was this some kind of cruel joke? To dangle the perfect man in front of my face after telling me to be matched to another? To point out all the flaws of the man meant for me and then keep everything I really wanted just out of reach? The moment I admitted to Chase my motives here, it would all disappear.

And yet.

When I thought of Ty, my mind could hardly picture the face I thought I knew so well. The only man I saw, the only one who counted, stood right here in front of me—and he started to lean in for a kiss, right before my disbelieving eyes.

For the second time today, Chase stopped just before his lips reached mine. His face hovered so close, I could feel the warmth of his skin and inhale the rich, musky island scent of him. I wanted to bury my face in his neck, wind my fingers in his hair, press our lips together and take our earlier kiss to a whole new level.

"Your call." His voice was so quiet the wind might have spoken it.

In that moment, I felt like two people—one who wanted to flee, and another who fought for control, screaming that I'd be stupid to ruin this and didn't I know better than the universe what I wanted? Didn't I deserve to seize happiness wherever I could find it? Wasn't Chase worth any risk? A kiss didn't mean marriage. It only meant two people found each other attractive.

So incredibly attractive. Chase was a massive chunk of magnetic metal, and I felt like a paper clip. The terrified part of me melted under the inevitable power of this man's allure, and suddenly she was gone as if she'd never existed.

I grabbed his head and pulled his lips down to mine.

He stiffened in surprise, and I felt his mouth curve into a grin before his hands took hold of my waist and pulled me closer, right up against him.

Fireworks. A forest fire. Nuclear explosions. I couldn't think of the right comparison for this. My kisses with Ty had been fun and addictive, but they didn't pick me up, smash me into the ground, whirl me around, and melt me into a puddle like Chase's did. Our moment earlier had been nothing compared to this. My entire body shook at the wonder of it.

He must have felt it too, because he groaned and lifted his hand to cup my cheek, pressing me even closer. Our limbs tangled together, as his kiss somehow intensified from one hundred to a thousand and beyond. I didn't know how my body remained standing. He probably held me up.

Finally, a millennia later, his kiss drew back into something more gentle, more tender. And then his lips pulled away, hovering just inches from my own, his eyes still closed.

"What did you do to me?" he asked softly, his voice rough.

I managed a soft chuckle. "I'd say I used my witch powers

to seduce you, but my legs are shaking too badly to make that convincing."

"I can carry you back to the car," he said, wearing a wolfish grin.

As tempting as being cradled by him would feel at this moment, the thought of being horizontal right now, my body pressed against his in any form, seemed like a very bad idea. We'd already taken this so far...my brain spun in oxygen-deprived disbelief at the very thought of it.

I'd just made out with Chase Everett. Not as a message or a demonstration, but because he liked me and I liked him. And it was by far the most incredible, mind-blowing kiss of my life.

"I'll float out of here under my own power, thank you very much." I winked, and he laughed.

We started back along the trail toward the car. But before I could get far, I felt his hand close on mine, encompassing the entirety of it. It felt firm, sure, and warm, sending another wave of heat and desire shooting through my body.

He's only holding your hand, I reminded myself, but it felt like downplaying a hurricane to a hailstorm.

Like it or not, Chase had taken control—and I no longer had any desire to fight it.

TWENTY-TWO

THE NEXT MORNING, after a short night's sleep following a busy and stressful rehearsal dinner that I'd basically floated through, I woke to a series of rapid knocks on my door. I stumbled in the darkness, unlocked the door, and peeked through the crack.

A hotel worker in a pristine white uniform peered back at me. "Breakfast, ma'am."

I pulled the door open enough to take the tray from his hands, not comprehending. "I didn't order breakfast."

He shrugged. "You were on the list. I'm supposed to give you this too." He placed a flower on the tray and hurried away.

A pink orchid, the same shade as Chase's pink sand beach. I lifted the flower to my nose and drew in the slightest scent of fresh island air, smiling a bit as I thought about yesterday. Had that really happened?

I glanced at the sofa and its pile of discarded pillows and the popcorn kernels on the floor that I still hadn't vacuumed.

Two paths. Two guys. I'd stepped onto one path and really

liked it. That didn't mean I couldn't still choose the other. Ty would get married the day after tomorrow. A few more feet along this path, and then I'd make a decision. Just a girl trying on jackets to see which fit best. No big deal.

When I brought the tray to the table to dig in, I noticed the corner of folded paper beneath the plate. Grinning, I opened it to read.

The tacos were good, but I can do better. Meet me at the hotel restaurant at 8p.m.

Uh oh. The hotel restaurant was black tie, very expensive. The gray dress I'd worn the other night would never do. Where would I find a dress suitable for the fanciest restaurant I'd ever set foot inside?

P.S. If you need something, COLOGIUE in town has a limited selection of formalwear. They've been advised to take good care of you.

Chase knew how exactly much money I made. Ever thoughtful, he was removing the financial burden of accepting his invitation. He had no idea how much I appreciated that. Every penny I earned this summer would have to go toward my rent in New York. Ironic, that I lived here in paradise for free while paying for a space I wasn't even occupying. Yet I had to make plans for the future.

The future.

Everything I did felt bent toward that goal, that one all-important word, and I didn't even know which future I was working toward.

❤ ❤ ❤ ❤ ❤ ❤

The waiter led me to Chase's table, where I enjoyed seeing Chase's eyes widen as I approached. His eyes swept down my body, betraying nothing as he stood to pull my chair out for me. I sat quickly and let him ease the chair forward, feeling his gaze on me all the while. Something inside me shivered from the heat I felt there.

As he took his seat across from me, still staring in unmasked admiration, I couldn't decide whether I wanted to know his thoughts or wanted to remain blissfully unaware.

If donning formalwear meant seeing Chase's unusually raw expression directed at me, I would wear a dress every day for the rest of my life.

"I have to disagree with you," he said, his voice strangely husky. "You are definitely the fancy dress type."

I didn't know what to say to that, so I changed the subject. "Sorry I'm so late. It's been a day."

Chase shook his head. "I heard about the bats. It's me who should be apologizing to you. We really need to get those under control."

I shuddered. The kitchen had suddenly become overrun with bats, which I shouldn't have had to deal with except it meant some of tonight's event food had to be tossed out. Luckily, the kitchen facilitator and I had worked out a deal with a local restaurant to fill in the gaps. I hadn't eaten since that glorious breakfast, and I couldn't wait to fill my empty stomach. "Not my favorite day."

He took my hand and cradled it in his. "You'd never know it by looking at you tonight. Is that a Ferra Rougée?"

I chuckled. "To be honest, I have no idea." I'd chosen the first gown to make the dress shop owner gasp, figuring she knew more than I did. It hadn't even required alterations, an apparently rare occurrence. The black velvet fabric seemed deeper and darker than most blacks, somehow, and the cut was something I'd never seen before—a full sleeve to my wrist on one side and sleeveless on the other, showing off my bare shoulder. The long slit revealed my entire left leg on the same side, and the gown extended down to the floor. I felt like a movie star.

"I can't tell you how refreshing that is." Chase looked up at the waiter, who'd arrived in an immaculate tux and looked ready for the red carpet himself. "Two Les Santenots du Milieu, please." The waiter nodded and hurried away.

Chase had called out the elephant in the room, so I chose that moment to bring it into the spotlight. "None of my other clothes are named after people, either, just so you know. But if you ask me the name of every player on the NBA team that won the championship last year, or the stats for the QB who won the Super Bowl for the last four years, I've got you."

"Casey McCormick, and yes, I'm sure you would win that competition." His eyes twinkled in amusement, fixed on me as if nobody else in the room existed. "After that epic volleyball game the other day, Casey is lucky that you never tried out for his position."

I shook my head. "I did kick twice for my high school football team after our kicker tore his hamstring. It was the scandal of the season. Alas, I missed both times. "

"Sounds like they should have given you a third try. Especially if you could kick in that dress and paralyze every pair of male eyes on the field. Poor, helpless fools." His hand extended to take mine, his thumb brushing across my knuckles.

Oh, I could touch him forever. The man sure cleaned up nice. As neat and tidy as his tuxedo looked, and despite how perfectly it accentuated his broad shoulders, it was Chase's hair that had me captivated. He'd combed it all forward and messed up the front in that intentional yet very sexy way guys used. I wanted to run my fingers through it.

Maybe I'd get a chance later.

I thought about him running his hands through *my* hair and felt a delighted shudder run through me. Could this truly be real?

A whisper behind me brought me back to reality. I couldn't pick out every word, but I definitely heard the words "new girl" and "wedding planner."

I didn't give them the satisfaction of looking over my shoulder to see if they were referring to me. The glares of the couple behind Chase's back told me enough. My presence had obviously created a stir. How could they possibly know who I was? I hadn't spoken with a single one of them.

Chase leaned forward. "Don't mind them. The snobbies never approve of a newcomer."

Said as if he weren't one of them. Which he wasn't, I knew now. Not at heart.

"Wait," I said, suddenly looking around at the empty table. "There's no menu."

"They only serve one meal each night, and it's always incredible. I brought the chef in from Peru. He's heralded as one of the best in the world."

"I look forward to it," I said, meaning every word. "I've only gotten three chapters into the first thriller you gave me, but I'm really liking it so far. I'm not just saying that."

"There are no cowboys and train chase scenes, unfortunately, but I think you'll find the ending riveting."

"It's already riveting. The hero is attractive in my head, so that helps. He's got these striking dark brown eyes and an obsession with his sunglasses, and he's tall like a football player and a little grumpy. Kind of like someone else I know."

"Agwe's only grumpy in the morning when he stays up too late." Chase winked.

I laughed. He squeezed my hand again, and oh, man. Even

that sent a shockwave of awareness through me. I forced myself to look away as the conversation continued, fully aware of the power this man had over me when he looked deep into my eyes.

New girl, indeed. I didn't know how many other "girls" he'd dined with here, nor did I want to know. But I did know that one hundred percent of his attention was now focused on me, and I intended to enjoy every moment while it lasted.

The dinner turned out to be lobster seasoned with citrus and some kind of sweet sauce that made me want to fetch them more lobster from the ocean so I keep eating all night long. Chase seemed pleased with my reaction, and we ate until neither of us could stomach another bite.

I never got the chance to offer to help pay, as Chase simply stood and pulled me to my feet. As we made our way to the elevator, I chided myself. As the owner, of course he wouldn't need to hand over his credit card. This entire restaurant existed because of him.

Neither of us wanted to go home yet, so we walked lazily to the beach. I removed my expensive heels—also chosen by the dress shop staff—and left them on a lounge chair next to his shiny black shoes. Then we walked in the sand together, hand in hand, in the moonlight. The wind tugged a curl free from the pinned pile atop my head and tossed it into my eyes. Chase halted, hooked it with a single finger, and tucked it behind my ear before I had the chance.

"I can see why so many people want to get married here," I murmured. "It's the most romantic place I've ever seen." Not that I'd ever been anywhere but New York and home, but I couldn't imagine anything better than this. Even if better beaches existed, they didn't have Chase—and that made all the difference.

"I'm glad you think so," he said, searching the shore. Before

I knew what had happened, he swept me into his arms and kissed me deeply.

I practically went limp before coming to my senses and wrapping my arms around his neck, pulling him even closer.

If fireworks didn't explode all around us, it certainly felt like it. This took yesterday's kiss to an entirely new level. My veins buzzed from the wine earlier and the intoxication of his lips on mine, tasting like sweet lobster and peppermint and the fresh air of his tropical island paradise. Just when I could stand it no longer, his lips left my mouth and left a trail across my jaw and down my throat, his hand still intertwined in my hair.

I wanted to pull him down, down, and even more down until we found ourselves tangled in the sand.

He must have been thinking along the same lines, because his free hand slid down around my waist, pulling my hips against his and his mouth crashed onto mine again. Were we vertical? Horizontal? I couldn't tell, our limbs all intertwined like this.

Okay, this wasn't just a new level. This was a new planet altogether. I'd never wanted someone so desperately.

I opened my eyes for the slightest of seconds and saw movement in the trees.

Chase must have felt me stiffen, because he pulled away and looked behind us.

"I thought I saw someone," I admitted reluctantly, barely able to get the words out. My heart sprinted a marathon in my chest, and my body surged with heat and wanting. Maybe it was good having somebody spying on us. It would prevent me from making a very public mistake.

"I should probably take you home anyway." I heard the same reluctance and breathlessness in his own voice. He slid one hand along my back and around my waist, and we walked across the beach together to fetch our shoes.

As I slid the second shoe on, I saw it again—a face in the trees. Only this time, I recognized the face.

The pool man.

TWENTY-THREE

I SAT BACK in my chair with a sigh before beginning the poem over again.

> No man is an island entire of itself; every man
> is a piece of the continent, a part of the main;
> if a clod be washed away by the sea, Europe
> is the less, as well as if a promontory were, as
> well as any manner of thy friends or of thine
> own were; any man's death diminishes me,
> because I am involved in mankind.
> And therefore never send to know for whom
> the bell tolls; it tolls for thee.

I'd found this online, searching for something else as I sipped my morning coffee, and immediately thought of Chase. If anyone qualified as an island, it would be Chase Everett with his dark sunglasses and gruff demeanor. A measure of protection from people who saw him as an opportunity? A calculated distance to ensure he never became his uncle? I couldn't say, and I really wanted more time to find out.

My phone buzzed with a text. Bridget. *Hey, lady. You awake yet?*

Grinning, I texted my reply. *For you? Always. How's boring old Arkansas?*

Missing you. How's it going with your mission to win back Ty? Has he kissed you yet?

I practically giggled, remembering that I hadn't updated her in a couple of days. Amazing how much could change in that time.

Actually, I wrote back, *I kinda switched to Chase. It's a long story.*

A pause, then: *What does that mean exactly? Don't tell me you're kissing Chase then.*

I didn't know how to respond to that, so I sent back a wink emoji instead.

She got it instantly. I could almost hear her squeal halfway around the world. *Seriously???* she shot back. *Is he a good kisser?*

Better than good, I told her.

I bet. Better than Ty, tho? He's the standard you compare everyone else to, so that's the ultimate test.

She was absolutely right about that. I'd compared Chase and Ty almost constantly in the past twenty-four hours, and Ty came up short every time.

Way better than Ty. No comparison.

There was a long pause before Bridget came back. *Sorry, Pops needed something. OK, I'm totally doing a browser search on Chase. If he has any dirt, we need to know it pronto because you, girl, are obviously smitten beyond repair.*

I frowned, but she was right. Better to have all the facts now rather than later. *How is Pops doing, anyway?*

Not so good these days, but I don't want to talk about that. I'm calling you, k?

My phone rang almost instantly. I answered in a second and heard a scream on the other end. I had to hold the phone away from my ear until it ended.

"What was that for?" I asked, barely holding back a laugh.

"That's the scream you deserve after news like this. Don't worry, Pops can't hear anyway. Okay, I'm pulling up some articles. They look pretty tame so far. Dude. Chase wears a lot of suits, doesn't he?"

I grinned. "You have no idea."

"I'm going to pretend that was an innocent comment. Wait, you guys haven't, like, gone further than kissing, right?"

"Bridget! Of course not."

"Just checking. I mean, this seems like a pretty new thing and you were dead-set on Ty just yesterday. Maybe you still are." She paused. "Are you?"

I hesitated. Was I? If I planned on stealing Ty, I wouldn't be dating Chase. But what if this thing with Chase ended just after Ty's wedding and then I couldn't have either of them? "I don't know."

"You don't *know?* Daphne, do I need to come out there and talk some sense into you?"

"I've got this. I just don't know where my head is yet."

"Sounds like it isn't your head that needs sorting out. I thought you had a plan. The fortune cookie? The horoscope? The plan to steal the groom right out from underneath that bratty bride's perfect nose?"

"Yes, and I did. I do. I think."

"Dang. He *must* be a good kisser." She cut off. "Oh."

"Oh, what?"

"Hang on a sec." She went silent for about a minute, then

whistled, low and slow. "Daph, I hate to be a downer, but you should see this." My phone buzzed.

I opened the link on the screen and read the headline.

BILLIONAIRE CHASE EVERETT ACCUSED OF STEALING FORTUNE FROM DYING UNCLE

"You know what? I have to go," Bridget said. "Sounds like Pops is in the kitchen again, and that always spells disaster. Read that article and text me when you're ready to talk. I'm always here for you, okay?"

"Okay," I said softly, my stomach feeling a bit unsettled at the seriousness in her voice.

We hung up and I began to read. Soon I found myself hugging my knees against my chest, staring at the photo at the bottom of the article, its cruel accusations ringing in my ears.

A distant family member had accused Chase of manipulating his uncle into changing the will to make him the sole heir. Since the change had been witnessed only by two medical workers and not notarized, the family member had challenged his fortune in court. The judge had awarded in favor of Chase, but the damage had already been done. The family had ostracized Chase, disowning him and trying to destroy every bit of wealth he had. They'd even tried to block the purchase of the island, but in the end, Chase had held on. Barely.

This version of the story didn't sound at all like the story he'd told me the other day. Could Chase be misleading me as much as I misled him? The thought cut deep.

I had to find out more. The article didn't name his accuser so I couldn't ask them for details, but I knew one person on the island who would possibly know the truth. I would confront him today. Now, before I saw Chase or anyone else.

I shot off a quick text to Bridget about getting back to her later, then hurried to take a shower.

♥ ♥ ♥ ♥ ♥

"Didn't think I'd see you again," the pool man muttered when I approached.

I didn't ask what that meant. We'd had two conversations before he found me kissing Chase in the darkness on the beach, our hands all over each other. He probably saw me as a traitor, and maybe rightly so. "I came to ask what you know about Chase."

He turned, putting his weight into the net pole. "If you're in his bed, isn't it a little late for that?"

I bristled. "I'm not in his bed, and even if I were, that wouldn't be any of your business."

"Then leave me to mine, because I am not losing my job." He turned back to the pool and scooped up a floating insect.

I'd handled this all wrong. With a sigh, I went to the pool shed and retrieved a second net. Then I started cleaning out the pool right along with him.

"What you saw," I told him. "That was completely unplanned. I didn't expect to be attracted to him, and I don't think he expected to be attracted to me either."

"I know a desperate attempt at job security when I see it," he grumbled. "I will not reveal my secrets so you can tell him and get me fired."

I glared down at him, my voice firm. "First of all, I am not manipulating Chase to keep my job. That's disgusting. Second of all, whatever you tell me is between us. It's just that I need to know everything before I let things progress any farther."

He gave me a sideways look. "You didn't believe me about him before, so why would you now?"

A tourist walked by with a blue-and-white-striped towel under her arm, so I waited for her to pass and lowered my voice to a whisper. "I found an article about the accusations against him. You know, manipulating his dying uncle to get his fortune. Did that really happen?"

The pool man looked torn. He glanced from one side of the pool area to the other, then gestured to the pool shed. I followed him and started stacking the pool nets on the wall.

"They're not accusations," he said quietly. "They're facts. I talked to the cousin who sued him when he visited a few months ago. He had evidence, but Chase's attorneys got the evidence thrown out in court. I'm telling you, Chase didn't win because he was in the right. He won because he had all the money in the world for the best attorneys and buying off witnesses. His uncle told everyone that Chase wouldn't get a cent, and suddenly the uncle's dead and Chase gets all the money? Seems suspicious to anyone with half a brain."

It did seem odd, when he put it that way. But there were two sides to every story...weren't there?

The pool man suddenly ducked into the shed. I stared at him in confusion before realizing he was hiding. In the distance, Chase emerged from the hotel with another man. He spotted me and waved me over.

I didn't want to meet his friend. I wanted to confront Chase, get the truth. I needed to see what he was hiding right now, not put on another girlfriend performance.

Although it wouldn't be a performance this time. But still.

I returned the net to its hook in the shed and approached.

"Tanner, meet Daphne," Chase said when I arrived. "Daphne, Tanner is an old friend. We avoided college together."

"To your detriment and my benefit, I'm afraid," Tanner told him with a friendly smile. He turned to me and held out a hand. "Nice to meet you, Daphne."

Now that I saw Tanner head-on, I knew his face better than most. "Hold on—you're that guy on YouTube. The travel guy?"

Tanner's smile widened. "Yep, our time in Costa Rica got me addicted to learning about other cultures. I've been traveling ever since, and I'm lucky that my channel funds my expeditions."

"Whatever. I heard about the car," Chase said, nudging his friend in the shoulder. "Red, was it?"

"Anyway," Tanner prompted, looking sheepish. "Thought I'd check on my friend here. Is there anything I need to have a little chat with him about, Daphne? Somebody needs to keep him in line. He's a little different out here than he is back in New York, isn't he?"

That couldn't be more true. "Very. Why do you think that is?"

"Obviously because you're here," Tanner said, picking up my hand and kissing the back of it. "Very pleased to meet you. Here's my card, if you need anything at all." He handed me a business card.

"Okay, Romeo," Chase growled, edging himself between us. "I know you're newly single, but I have no qualms about taking you out on a fishing boat and throwing you overboard."

Out of the corner of my eye, I spotted Ty settling on a distant lounge chair near the pool, watching us.

Tanner laughed. "Just messing with you both. I have no intention of dating anytime soon. I'm married to my work, and she has a lot to offer. No complaints."

Chase's expression softened. "Yeah, I heard about your last experience. Sorry, man."

"Sometimes things happen for a reason. Guess it wasn't

meant to be. You two, though—you'd better invite me to the wedding if this works out, okay? I'm going to make a phone call really quick." Tanner strode off toward the beach, pulling out his phone.

"Does he drop in often?" I asked Chase.

"A few times a year," he said, hooking my waist and pulling me against him. "Tanner loves this island almost as much as I do. I should have warned you. He can be a bit over the top sometimes."

"I guess that's why his audience loves him." I hesitated, pulling away to look at him. "Um, do you have a second to talk? I wanted to ask you about something."

He glanced after his friend. "Sure, I have a minute or two."

A worker approached. "Sorry to disturb you, Mr. Everett. You have another visitor waiting in the lobby."

Chase smacked his forehead. "I thought she wasn't coming till tomorrow. I'm sorry, Daphne. Can it wait until later?"

I forced a smile. "Of course."

He and the worker strode off together, talking in low tones.

Ty appeared at my side. "Daphne, are you okay? You look troubled. Did something happen?"

I turned to look at the man I'd once loved, who stared back with a frown. This should have been the perfect moment to talk to him, to have the conversation I'd come here to initiate. Yet I had no desire to discuss Chase with him right now.

"I'm fine," I lied. "Where's Veronica?"

"Tanning. Seriously, Daphne. You look like someone just died. There must be something I can do." He paused. "Actually, here. These always did cheer you up." He grabbed a plastic-wrapped fortune cookie from his backpack and shoved it into my hand.

I stared at it. Since when did Ty carry fortune cookies

around? Where had he even gotten this? I didn't recall seeing any Chinese restaurants on the island.

Was this some kind of bizarre sign from the universe? Because I was *not* interested right now.

Ty leaned forward. "I'm here if you want to talk."

I gave a bitter laugh. His rehearsal dinner was tonight. "No, you aren't, but that's the way it should be. I really do hope you and Veronica find happiness."

I turned and headed toward the lobby, leaving him gaping in bewilderment.

TWENTY-FOUR

CHASE PROVED DIFFICULT TO FIND. I spent at least twenty minutes looking for him and asked several workers, none of whom knew anything of his whereabouts. He didn't answer his texts or the radio either. Odd.

I finally found him down by the beach, talking to a woman with a slight build and brassy blonde hair. I was at least fifty feet away when he and the woman started laughing. She lifted a hand to his arm and gripped it in a very friendly way, and he didn't move it.

I slowed.

Her hand sat there for several seconds. The smile he wore at that moment, easy and free, was the one I'd thought reserved only for me.

Now I stood there, frozen like a fool, for several seconds before diving behind yet another cluster of tropical bushes.

Through the branches, I saw her hand slide even further up his arm and around his back, pulling against him in an embrace. His arms wrapped around her tightly and they stood there for a long moment, the wind whipping her hair against his neck.

I turned around and found a bench to sit on, unable to look any longer. The hard, heavy feeling in the pit of my stomach felt too soft now, like it wanted to crawl back up my esophagus and escape for good.

Tourists walked by on the sidewalk, giving me curious glances, but I didn't dare stand until Chase and that woman had finished their little moment. I imagined myself stalking up to him with fire in my eyes, accusing him of cheating on me. But you had to be together for there to be accusations of cheating, and I couldn't even say what we were. Did he have other women on this island, all of whom he shared makeout sessions with but didn't commit to beyond that?

At that moment, Chase and the woman appeared on the walkway, headed in the direction of the hotel. His face brightened when he saw me sitting there. "Daphne. There you are. I have another introduction to make."

The woman grinned as she looked me over, and I realized that she was more mature than she'd appeared from a distance. Wrinkles pulled at her eyes, which were a luminescent blue. She had to be at least thirty years older than either of us.

"Aunt Carolle," Chase said too formally, "meet Daphne. We're thrilled you made it a day early."

We. As if he and I were both hosting her. I felt like a complete fool. "How nice to meet you, Carolle."

The woman wrapped me in a hug, just like she had with Chase. "I've only been here five minutes and Chase has already told me all about you. Seems you've captured my nephew's heart, so you must be a special one."

"I'm not sure about that, but thank you." I smiled graciously at the compliment and turned back to Chase. "I didn't realize you had an aunt."

"Carolle is my uncle's youngest sister," Chase explained. "She lives in Kansas."

"I wasn't in a position to take in poor Chase back then, or heaven knows I would have. He deserved far better than my brother ever gave him." She leaned in conspiratorially. "And if you make a joke about me not being in Kansas anymore, I just might throw sand at you."

I liked her already. "Heard that joke a few times?"

"It's only funny the first five hundred times. After that, you want to strangle people. There's more to Kansas than a movie with red slippers and yellow sidewalks. We also have some pretty incredible gas stations." She winked.

I belted a laugh before I could help it. "Those don't receive nearly enough credit. Especially the ones with clean bathrooms."

"She speaks truth," Carolle told Chase. "I approve."

"So do I." Chase watched me with a proud smile.

In a moment, everything came rushing back. The inheritance. His family's accusations.

"There's just one problem here," Carolle said. "You haven't greeted your girl properly, Chase. Give her a kiss or two, and then you can show me to my room. Left my baggage in the lobby with a bewildered worker wielding a mop, and it's nap time anyway."

"Yes, ma'am." Chase turned me around to face him. Seconds later, his mouth found mine. As much as I wanted to let it linger, I shortened the kiss and kept it nice and chaste with his aunt watching.

We just fit so well together. How could something feel so right and yet be so wrong?

I turned back to Carolle. "I should, um, get back to work. It was nice to meet you."

The woman beamed. "Very pleased to meet you too, Daphne."

I gave Chase one last look, noting the tightness of his eyes as he watched me. He must have felt my hesitation in that kiss. Then I strode quickly away.

My questions would have to wait for another time.

When I reached my office and opened Ty's fortune cookie a few minutes later, I couldn't decide whether to study it or throw it across the room.

You're on the right path.

Right. That would be more helpful if I knew which path I was actually on.

I spent most of Ty and Veronica's rehearsal dinner in the kitchens, keeping busy supervising orders. I caught a glimpse of Chase once and our gazes met, but he didn't approach, likely sensing that I needed some space. I was the first to look away.

When I returned home late that night, I couldn't sit on the same couch I'd shared with Chase, nor could I eat in the kitchen Chase had stocked with food. Everywhere I looked, there he was.

So I channeled my inner eighteen-year-old, buried my fear, and climbed onto the tin roof.

Soon I lay on my back, arms crossed beneath my head, looking up at the massive black expanse of sky above. The stars glistened, some bright and others more faded, all situated in their respective places. How nice it would be to know where that was—to be acted upon by the forces of gravity and physics in predictable ways, never changing, no choice whatsoever in the matter. No weighing the happiness of others against their own. No guilt. Only obedience to laws as ancient as the universe.

Those stars had to be wiser than me. They'd been around far longer than I could comprehend. If they spoke, I had to listen. I had to trust that everything would work out the way it should.

Didn't I?

I'd spend most of my life following whatever direction from the universe I could find. Yet after all this time, I still hadn't found the happiness I sought. Maybe Mom was right about fate and destiny. I'd looked everywhere for answers except inside myself.

The problem was, I didn't have the answers, either. I'd seen a side of Chase that few others got to see, but how much of that was the truth? If I ignored the warning signs, would I regret rejecting what could be a warning from fate?

Only one thing could be done. I would ask Chase about those accusations the next time I saw him, no matter what. If he so much as blinked wrong, I'd know they were true and end it right then.

But Ty...could I even say I wanted to spend the rest of my life with him? Our differences hadn't gone away. He had four dozen guests in town for his wedding tomorrow, mostly family and friends excited to celebrate with him. Could I live with destroying their happiness to secure my own?

Could I be that person, no matter what the stars said?

There were voices down below.

I crawled to the edge of the roof and looked down to find Agwe and Ty at my front door.

"Thanks, man," Ty said, holding out a fistful of money.

Agwe stared at him, unblinking. "I do not need to be tipped, thank you. Daphne is my friend. So is Chase. Whatever your business here, may it be honorable for my friends."

Ty cleared his throat. "Sure, whatever. You take care now."

Agwe lingered a moment longer before disappearing into the trees.

Ty knocked on the door. I waited a few seconds before whispering. "You're going to need a ladder."

He looked upward and grinned. "Did I ever tell you that you're twelve at heart?"

"Twelve is on the generous side. Did you need something? How's Veronica?"

"Pouting at the moment, although that's pretty normal. Actually, I came to talk to you. You look mighty comfy up there, so looks like I'll have to overcome my fear of heights pretty quick."

I gripped the side of the tin roof, careful not to cut myself on the sharp edge. "If you can make it up here without breaking your neck, you've earned one conversation."

He looked around at the trees, all too far from the roof for assistance. "How did you get up there, anyway?"

"No hints."

"I suppose calling 'Rapunzel, Rapunzel, let down your hair' won't work this time, huh?"

"Nope."

He sighed. "You really won't come down?"

"Not a chance." I made my way back to the center, lay on my back, and crossed my arms under my head once more, but the peace had fled the instant Ty had arrived. Now I felt on edge, an impatient buzzing in my veins. I wanted Ty to have his say and then leave again. Or better yet, just leave. The stars and I had a few things to work out, and I couldn't do that with Ty muddling my mind.

A week ago, you were ready to marry him, I reminded myself, and I couldn't refute that.

A series of grunts penetrated the night air. A moment later, Ty's face appeared in the tree. He grabbed hold of the roof, climbed onto it, and then carefully crawled my direction. He held himself as if the roof would collapse at any moment.

Soon he lay on his back next to me, looking up at the stars. "Bright here, aren't they?"

"Yeah."

"Much clearer than in New York." He turned his head to look at me. "Seems like everything is."

My stomach felt all murky again. Not here. He couldn't possibly be starting this conversation on my roof, the night before his wedding.

"I've been a fool," he said, "and I need you to forgive me."

I allowed myself a glance at him in the darkness, the moonlight illuminating half his face, and I saw only truth there. A truth I'd wanted to see there for a very long time.

"Our breakup really messed with my head," he continued. "Veronica was there when I needed her, and I'll always be grateful for that. But lately, she and I have been growing apart. I'm realizing that my biggest mistake wasn't dating you, but letting you go. We had something special, and I didn't realize how special until you were gone for good. When I saw you in that lobby, all those feelings came back. I think you felt it too." His hand found mine.

I pulled my hand away and folded my hands on my stomach, still looking upward at the sky. "Ty, your wedding is tomorrow. This is your nerves talking."

"If that's the case, it's the first time I've thought clearly in months. Maybe longer. You didn't answer my question. That day, in the lobby. Tell me you felt it too. If you didn't, I'll go."

I swallowed. Hard. My entire future felt split in two, a fork in the road that I could no longer avoid. My next words would determine which road to take, and there would be no turning back.

One road was meant to be mine, dictated by the stars. Determined by the universe that had brought me into being.

And the other seemed too light, too impossibly perfect, to be real. A shimmering mirage in the desert. A happiness that someone like me couldn't possibly hope to deserve, not in a thousand lifetimes.

"I felt it," I whispered.

The roof creaked as he rose onto his elbow and looked down on me. His breath was hot in the warm breeze. It smelled of tropical chewing gum.

"Do you feel it now?" he asked softly. I felt his leg leaning against mine.

"You're asking me this tonight?" I laughed incredulously at the bizarre nature of this conversation. "You've already made your decision. You're marrying an heiress in a matter of hours."

He must have heard the strain in my voice, because he watched me for a long moment, as if waiting for the second part of my answer. When it didn't come, he said, "And you're dating a billionaire."

I didn't answer, unable to confirm nor deny the fact. We'd never really discussed our level of commitment. At the very least, he was my fake boyfriend, so I should have agreed with his statement, right? But after all the lies I'd told over the past few weeks, I didn't have it in me to tell even one more.

"I can see you have doubts," he continued. "I mean, how well do you really know Chase? Rumors can exaggerate the circumstances, but they're usually rooted in some kind of truth. You may not have a college degree, but even you can do research. How much research have you done on Chase, Daphne? Tell me that."

Even me? What was that supposed to mean? My walls shot up. "I know that he makes me happy." And for once, I didn't feel a stab of guilt at the admission. Chase truly did offer a happiness I'd never known before, not even with Ty.

Could I be happy once I discovered the truth about his past?

Ty leaned even closer, his lips hovering just over mine. "You make *me* happy," he whispered. "I'm not letting that billionaire steal you away from me. Not when you're within reach."

"Ty, you broke up with me. You chose Veronica." My voice felt pitifully small.

"I'm unchoosing her and choosing you. You're the one I want. I just had to be reminded of that. Please give me a chance." His lips closed the distance between us, and it took me far too long to realize that we were kissing. Our mouths moved together exactly as they had over a year before, so comfortable and familiar, like a worn couch.

A pickle-green 70s couch with the stuffing poking out and fleas. With disco music playing in the background and bright orange carpet beneath it. Groovy and retro, but not somewhere I wanted to spend a lot of time. Definitely not somewhere I wanted to spend the rest of my life.

Still on one elbow, he pressed me harder against the tin roof. Any second, he would swing his leg over mine. I knew how this would go if I didn't stop it.

I'd stepped a foot on one road only to find it crumbling beneath my feet. I had to explore the other road first. I had to know if things with Chase could possibly work out before... settling for this. And *settling* was exactly the right word— because now that I'd kissed both men, I knew that what Ty and I had enjoyed wasn't magic. It wasn't even remarkable. It was convenient, and little more.

I managed to turn my head and break the kiss before scrambling to a sitting position. "Look, you're right, okay? I did feel something. But I'm not sure I do now."

Ty lifted a hand in surrender. "Daphne, you were meant to be mine. I know it. We took a little detour, the both of us, but things are as they should be now. Whatever's holding you back, we'll leave it far behind us when we leave this island tonight."

Whoa there, tiger. "Tonight? I—I don't—"

"Yes, you do. There's nothing here that really matters. They'll all understand when we go missing in the morning."

Now I felt physically ill. "You want to sneak off without telling anyone?"

"It's easier that way. Less drama. I have a friend in New York whose place is empty for the summer. I can talk him into letting us stay there for a few nights. That's all the time we need to get the marriage license and find your ring."

"My ring?" Mind whirling, I tried to bring reality back down to my brain. "Not a chance, Ty. I can't just leave Chase wondering what happened. I need to talk to him."

"So he can talk you out of it? Daphne, don't be a fool."

I rose to my feet, looking down on the man fate decreed I should marry. "I'm not a fool. I need time. This is a huge decision."

"Time is one thing I don't have a lot of, but I'll tell you what. Take the morning to get your affairs in order. Confront Chase about his past. Get everything out in the open so you feel good about this, because I do. There's a flight out at 1:45 p.m. I'll be waiting in the lobby at noon with a car and two plane tickets." He rose to his feet as well. Stepping carefully, he made his way over and planted a quick kiss. "This is exactly as it should be. You'll see that soon enough."

The night air was warm, but I shivered. "I'll let you know."

"You don't have to. Just show up so I can sweep you away." He leaned in again.

This time, I dodged the kiss. "I think you should go. I don't know how strong this roof is."

He jerked, suddenly looking nervous. "How do I get down?"

I almost wanted to see him try to climb back down the tree, but that would take forever and put his safety at risk. So I lifted the hatch I'd come through and motioned to the ladder. "Much easier."

He chuckled. "Smooth. I'll see you tomorrow night."

All I heard was shuffling, footsteps on the main floor, the door opening and closing, and then whistling...until the whistling stopped abruptly.

I looked over the edge to find Chase and Ty on my front walk, staring each other down.

Ty ducked and hurried toward the path leading to the resort. Chase must have felt my gaze on him, because he found me on the rooftop. As our eyes locked, the world seemed to freeze around us. A world of emotion lay bare in his eyes, hurt and bewilderment and all the betrayal I'd tried so hard to avoid.

I wanted to defend myself, to explain Ty's presence here. But my traitorous mouth refused to speak. How could I tell the truth when even that contained so many lies?

Finally, he turned and disappeared into the shadows.

TWENTY-FIVE

I spent the next two hours calling and texting Chase, but it all went straight to voicemail. I didn't dare use the radio with others listening in, and I didn't know whether he lived in a bungalow or a hotel suite, much less the location. So I spent a long night tossing and turning, determined to find him the moment the sun came up.

But the next morning, he was nowhere to be found. A phantom.

Every time somebody told me they'd spotted him, he would be gone before I arrived. I knew exactly what that meant, and it created a sick feeling inside at the memory of the horror and realization in his eyes.

He'd likely had a sleepless night too.

I finally gave up searching the grounds and decided to search the perimeter, in the thicker part of the trees. A trail led off toward the resort entrance off the pool area, so I decided that was as good a place to start as any. But as I got deeper into the shadows of the canopy, it wasn't a man's voice I heard, but a woman's. A voice I knew all too well.

I dove behind a cluster of trees and slowly peered around them. Veronica paced along the trail with a sparkly phone to her ear, a furious expression on her pretty face.

"I think you're forgetting that I'm the one doing all the work here," she was saying.

Veronica paused to listen and then laughed. Her laugh sounded like a dainty drill on stubborn concrete. "Daddy, I can always marry the guy. Then you'd be in a pinch, wouldn't you? No resort, paying the full event fee, *and* a useless son-in-law. Remember, I'm the one in charge here. We do it my way or not at all."

I plastered myself against one of the trees, not daring to breathe. Do *what* her way or not at all? Why would she be talking to her father over the phone and not in person? Wasn't the guy already here for his daughter's wedding? The questions came thicker and faster.

"I told you, I deserve half. You don't know what it's like, looking these people in the eye and pretending this wedding is going to happen. And convincing Ty that I'm a blushing bride and head over heels in love with him? Daddy, seriously. I'm the one selling my soul for this. At least fifty percent or the deal's off."

I gritted my teeth, trying to make sense of her words. Anyone could tell she cared more about herself than she did about Ty, but this? Pretending to be in love and faking a marriage for the sake of some business deal?

Chase had been desperate enough to sign a bad contract with Marcus and Kamia's wedding, and he'd quite literally paid the price. Had he made the same deal for Ty and Veronica's? If so, her calling it off would certainly be the final nail in the coffin.

Even Chase had admitted that Veronica's dad wanted the resort and the island. *Clever*, he'd called her, when musing about why Veronica would choose him to host the event after their rocky history. It all made sense.

"Thank you, Daddy." Veronica's voice was sugar-sweet now. "I knew you'd see it my way. Stay tuned for an update after tonight's event. It will be the performance of my life." She hung up, checked her appearance on her phone's camera, and practically skipped away.

Veronica had come with the intention of destroying Chase's company. How could she lead Chase on for so long and then drop such a devastating bombshell when she'd once cared for him? And how could she use Ty like this, who didn't deserve any of it?

Same reason you're doing it to Chase, a voice said from deep inside. Veronica was positioning herself for the future. I wasn't much better than Veronica right now, and I couldn't deny that.

I did know one thing for sure. Chase had to know about this, and fast.

❤ ❤ ❤ ❤ ❤

I finally spotted him at the pool, speaking with a female worker there. I didn't see the balding pool cleaner anywhere.

The moment Chase spotted me, his shoulders tensed and his expression hardened. No arm extended to greet me, no smile. He looked practically ready for war when I reached his side.

"Thanks for the update," Chase told the worker.

"Anytime, Mr. Everett." The woman looked between the two of us warily and hurried off, probably sensing the impending storm.

Chase said nothing. He didn't even look at me—simply started walking away.

"We need to talk," I said, hurrying after him. "Chase, please."

It took me two strides for every one of his. I finally caught up to him on the beach. He stood there in his sandals, not bothered by the waves devouring his feet, staring at the horizon.

"I keep fooling myself," he muttered.

I clamped my mouth shut, stifling the speech I'd planned, and forced myself to listen.

He shook his head in disbelief. "Every time. Every single freaking time, yet I keep stupidly believing it will end better."

The pain on his face sent a new ache reverberating through my chest. I reached up to touch his arm as I had a hundred times. He recoiled from my touch.

"I know you think I betrayed you—" I began.

He jerked away, tense and frustrated. "More than anyone else ever has."

Chase may as well have slapped me, because that one hurt. "And we can talk about that, but there's something you need to know first. It's about Veronica."

Chase's expression darkened. "You got back together with your ex, and you think I want to talk about Veronica right now?"

"I did not! Well, there was a kiss, but I ended it and sent him away. I only meant that you were right about Veronica, or at least sort of right, that she's using Ty to get back at you. I heard her talking on the phone just now—"

"Daphne, stop trying to distract me from you and Ty, and tell me the truth." Chase's tone sounded injured. "I need to know how long this has been going on. When did you finally give in, and when were you going to tell me? The full truth."

I paused, a sinking feeling in the pit of my stomach. Chase

wouldn't listen to my warning until he had the full picture. The time for secrets was over. He deserved that much.

"Ty broke it off a year ago, but I never stopped loving him," I admitted. "When I saw him at the office back in New York, I felt this raging jealousy. I couldn't let that woman have him. And my horoscope said we were meant to be together, and so did that fortune cookie, so I—"

"Fortune cookie?" He looked incredulous.

I plunged on before I lost my nerve. "Anyway, I felt I'd been called to this mission, to steal him back. That's why I accepted this job. I intended to win him over within the week and be long gone by now."

If eyes could be ice, his were icebergs. Big, deep, Titanic-sinking ones. He stared at me for a long moment as my words reshaped how he saw me, and I felt the reshaping in my bones. "You used me."

My throat squeezed. "At first, yes. Or I intended to. But—"

"Twice over. I brought you here to help me save the company, yet you planned on tanking it all along. And if that weren't enough, you had to tank me right along with it."

Tears stung my eyes now. "I never planned that part. Chase, you need to believe me. I was as surprised by our attraction as you were. It changed everything."

"It didn't change a thing, so don't pretend it did."

Every word felt like a knife aimed straight for the heart. I let my planned speech go and spoke from the soul. "Look, this is the biggest decision of my life."

"Decision?" He chuckled bitterly. "Let me do you a favor and remove one of the options. Problem solved." He turned to leave.

"Chase." My voice wobbled ever so slightly. "Veronica's here because her dad sent her. He wants her to call off the wedding so you're hit with the bill and have to declare bankruptcy. He plans to swoop in and take the resort."

He stopped, his back to me.

"I know you have no reason to believe me, but it's true. Ty doesn't know. I just barely overheard the conversation she was having on the phone, and I don't think she saw me hiding in the trees. Whatever you do, know that I care about you and what happens to you and the company."

Chase snorted. "Between you and Veronica, my company was never going to survive."

I flinched, then continued in a small voice. "I heard things about you, that your relationships never last because you have too many secrets. They say you manipulated your uncle in the hospital to change his will. I realized how little I knew about you. It spooked me."

He looked back at me, over his shoulder, wearing a wounded look. "And you believed them."

"Did you steal your uncle's money?" I asked in a small voice.

"You're right about one thing," he snapped. "You know absolutely nothing about me, and clearly I know even less about you." He stalked off.

"Chase, I only want to understand." I started to follow him.

"That makes one of us. I know all I need to know about you, Daphne. Now get off my island."

TWENTY-SIX

As I packed, I pondered my conversation with Chase. I wasn't sure what I had expected, but I definitely hadn't foreseen how much this would hurt. Not just getting fired, because I didn't care about that. There would always be other jobs. But there was only one Chase, and only one Isle de Pura Vida.

As much as being betrayed hurt, being the betrayer hurt a hundred times worse.

I finished packing, gave the room and pile of books on the bed one last glance, and resolved to leave and never look back just like I'd always planned to do. Chase had caught me red-handed. I had nothing to hide and nothing left to gain or lose. The glittering path of light and joy had been burned to a husk of what it had been before, yet I still found it hard to leave.

Then I realized why. Deep down, I knew I had to try to make this right. Completely mending the damage I'd caused would require time travel, but I could do something small and hope it made a difference.

Two conversations. One to resolve my past and another to

secure Chase's future. No matter what happened with my own, at least I could move on knowing I'd done all I could.

Ty responded to my text within seconds. *Praise God. I thought you were running.*

I am, I wrote back.

Silence.

Ty, I began. *Don't interrupt. You need to know that Veronica plans to dump you. I overheard her talking to her dad about using you to bankrupt Chase's company so he can swoop in and take the resort. You don't have to believe me, but it's true. I'm sorry. Second, I wanted to marry you for the longest time. At one point, you became the ultimate goal in my life, the standard against whom I compared other guys. I've moved on from that, but thank you. I'm glad we had something special for a while.*

There was a long pause. I almost thought he wouldn't write back, then the words appeared.

I can't believe you're staying with him.

Poor Ty. *I'm not,* I wrote back, *but that doesn't make a difference for you either. Go and find a good woman to marry. Someone who loves you and won't use you. You deserve better.*

Then I closed the conversation.

I gave myself about thirty seconds to feel this, to really experience the shock of change, of watching that first path fizzle into a blurry, overgrown forest. That path wasn't for me. Maybe it had been once, but not anymore. The fact that the second path had been burned to a blackened, smoking husk didn't change the mediocrity of the first one.

Ty wasn't mine.

I stuffed the bag of personal items from my office into the suitcase. At the last second, the Magic 8 ball rolled off the bed and hit the floor near my feet, as if taunting me. Tempting me. I picked it up for a long moment, considering.

Then I dumped it into the trash can.

Only one conversation left. I pulled a business card out of my pocket and typed the number into my phone.

"Hey Tanner," I said when he answered. "Chase would never admit it, but he needs your help."

♥ ♥ ♥ ♥ ♥

When my plane landed in New York, I didn't go to Everett Events. I had nothing there to retrieve, and I couldn't face the glares and whispers. Everyone would know what had happened by now. It would be a miracle if Chase didn't sick his lawyers on me, honestly. He had every right to try suing me, and for a woman with less than $50 to her name, I would be completely buried.

I hadn't seen Ty at the airport. Hopefully he'd confronted Veronica and gotten the truth from her own lips.

Instead, I went back to my apartment to pack. It was time to go home.

An hour later, I stood there, looking at my bed with the rest of the loft empty. It didn't feel like I'd thought it would. I'd expected to feel sad at the end of an era that had lasted almost seven years. But instead, I felt...powerful. Older. Taking my future into my hands felt really good, and I wasn't sure I could explain why.

I pulled out my phone to check the time just as it started ringing. Ty. I'd deleted his number after our breakup and added it again on the island using company records. Somehow, in the craziness of traveling, I'd forgotten to delete it again.

My deliberating lasted about three seconds. Just before his name disappeared and my phone sent him to voicemail, I answered. "Hey."

"Daphne. Please don't hang up."

A funny thing to say, since I'd answered the phone, but whatever. "This isn't a great time."

"Look, we didn't get to finish our conversation. You shared your side, but I didn't get to share mine. Can we meet tonight? Say, Heudon's around 9?"

"Ty, my bus leaves in an hour. I'm sorry."

"I thought you might say that, so I covered my bases. Actually, if you don't want to meet me for dinner, can you do me a favor and step outside your door for a second?"

Confused, I stared at my phone.

"Daphne, please. Trust me."

I didn't trust him. Not with my time, not with my heart. I was tired of playing his games.

"I'm going to keep asking until you do it," Ty said. "Two minutes, that's it."

The words came out in a half-growl. "You have two minutes." I stabbed the End button on my phone and started to make my way down the spiral staircase. A moment later, I yanked the front door open to find Ty on one knee, holding an open ring case with the biggest ring I'd ever seen.

Oh, no.

"Daphne," he said slowly.

The door across the hall opened slightly, and I saw the dark circle of a phone peek out. He'd paid my neighbor Roger to film this?

"I can't live without you," Ty said, sounding as if he recited something he'd memorized. "My life is darkness without your light, cold without your warmth, and misery without your happiness. I would be honored if you would—"

"Hey, that's from that one movie," Roger said, peeking his head further out his door. "You know, the one with the motorcycle chase on the cruise ship?"

Ty gritted his teeth. "Anyway, I was wondering if you'd be so kind—"

I tore the ring box from his hand. "This is Veronica's ring, isn't it?"

He looked flustered. "Well, yes, but now it's yours. If you want it."

Here it was, the moment I'd wanted for months. I had dreamed about words like this coming from his mouth more times than I could count. And yet, all of this felt fake. Like a mockery of what I really wanted.

Ty stood. "We're meant to be together, Daphne. It's right. Don't you feel it? Like fate itself wants us to be together?"

The fortune cookie. The horoscope. Even my best friend— and then there was Chase and the entire disaster with him. The fact that I had nowhere to go now but home. Everything pointed to Ty. If I accepted, I could stay in New York like I'd always planned.

But the Daphne who had wanted all those things—believed in all those things—no longer existed. I knew that now.

"I'm not letting fate decide my course anymore," I told him softly. "I'm making my own decisions now. I'm going home."

Ty's face went tense, and for a moment, I thought he would explode with anger. The Ty I'd once known might have. But for some reason, whether it was the fact that my neighbor had a camera or the very public nature of our conversation, he chose to simply nod and wrap me in a short hug.

"Thank you for telling me about Veronica," he said against my ear. "And good luck with everything." He turned and hurried away, shaking his head and muttering something about trying the pawn shop.

Roger stood gaping in his doorway, his phone still raised.

I watched as Ty made it to the end of the hallway and

stalked toward the stairs. He didn't even look back. If he had, it wouldn't have changed a thing.

My heart was no longer his, even if the man who had it now didn't want it.

I turned and went inside to say my last goodbyes.

❤ ❤ ❤ ❤ ❤

When I reached the bus station, I watched the bus driver toss my stuff in the storage compartment underneath and kept only my handbag, clutching it to my chest as I climbed up the steps and found a seat near the back. Strangely, I barely felt sad as I stared at the city I'd loved so long and so well, the place that had once held my hopes and dreams. I knew now that happiness could happen anywhere. It wasn't the place but the people I shared that place with that could fill me with joy.

The bus ride home lasted almost twenty-seven hours. My backside felt molded to the seat by the time we arrived, and my sleep-deprived brain struggled to get an Uber and concentrate on making it home.

The moment I stepped out of the car, however, everything snapped into focus.

Home.

I hadn't set eyes on this tiny farmhouse in so long. Not since storming out, shoving items into my bag as I waited for my friend to arrive and drive me to the airport.

Now here I stood, my suitcases a little fuller, my heels higher, my wallet lighter, and my heart more battered than ever.

"Thank you," I called to the Uber driver, who had set my

suitcases on the driveway while I stood there, staring at my house.

He sent me a wave and drove off.

The house looked smaller than I remembered, yet it shone almost as if from within. A new coat of light green paint glistened in the sun, and the door had been replaced recently with a less splintered version. Still solid wood though. Dad wouldn't settle for anything less.

I left my baggage on the sidewalk—just in case—and stepped carefully up the front walk to the door. A few quick raps with my knuckles, and I stood back to wait. How many times had I burst through this doorway, the master of my world and everything in it? Confident and happy?

The door opened a crack. Then I heard a gasp and it flew open wide, revealing my mother standing there. "Daphne."

"Hi, Mom," I said in a tight voice.

I'd barely gotten the words out when she threw her arms around me. No questions, no lectures. Just her arms and her love surrounding every part of me.

"I'm sorry," I whispered against her hair.

"Honey, you're right where you belong," my mother said fiercely. "No use being sorry for that."

TWENTY-SEVEN

I sat at a round dining table more familiar than almost anything in my life, admiring the woodwork of the heavy leg in the center. Simple on top yet intricate underneath, this table held plenty of memories. I recalled the many art projects and math homework sessions I'd both enjoyed and endured here as a child. How many dinner conversations had this table seen? How many discussions that later turned into arguments and then reconciliation?

Except for the one argument that had never been reconciled. The one when Dad had admitted his condition and I'd realized he'd been fighting cancer for weeks without my knowledge.

At the time, I'd felt justified in my anger. Now I knew it hadn't been anger at him or my mom, not really. Deep inside, I'd been angry with myself.

I'd been so absorbed in my own life, I hadn't seen my own father fighting for his.

"Grilled chicken and mashed potatoes," Mom called,

setting a pan onto one of her crocheted oven mitts in the center of the table. "Lots of butter, Daphne. Just how you like it."

"On the potatoes or the chicken?" Dad asked, taking his seat. He flashed me a tight smile.

Mom leaned down to kiss his cheek. "Both."

"Atta girl."

Soon we were all seated and looking around awkwardly. Mom finally cleared her throat and Dad got the hint, calling for a blessing on the food while we held hands. It seemed as familiar as birdsong, sitting here like this. So much better than scraping together random ingredients from the cupboard in my tiny apartment and calling it dinner.

"Oh, wow," I groaned after putting the first bite of potatoes into my mouth. "Was it always this good?"

"Not possible. Everything's better now that you're home." Mom winked and began to cut her meat.

Dad stared at his plate. "So are we going to talk about this or just keep pretending nothing's changed?"

"Dad," I moaned.

"Henry," Mom said, a warning tone in her voice.

Dad finally met my gaze. "It's just that you stormed out of this house almost seven years ago and haven't come back for anything. Not for Christmas, no birthdays, nothing. Wouldn't let us come visit you, either."

Mom gripped the table. "We spoke on the phone hundreds of times, and you wouldn't say a word."

"That's not what I meant," Dad said.

For the second time that week, I gathered my courage and stared him down. "You're right. I haven't been the daughter you both deserve."

He tipped his hand toward me as if to say, *There you go.*

I wasn't done. "But I also feel as if I haven't had a father for the past seven years, and that hurt. It hurt that you would keep your condition a secret and ask Mom to do the same. Secrets kill relationships, even when you're trying to protect someone. I've learned that the hard way." And they especially hurt when they only benefitted one person. I recalled the betrayal I'd felt the night I left home and remembered Chase's expression when he faced me on the beach a few days before. It wasn't all that different.

Dad's eyes lowered. "I never meant to hurt you, baby girl, but I see your point. Don't be angry with your mom. This one's on me."

"I'm not angry with either of you. I've come a long way since I left. I didn't know a whole lot about myself or what I wanted back then. The only dream I had was New York, and leaving finally gave me the courage to pursue it. I'm not sure I would have gone if we hadn't argued."

Dad nodded. "And now? Is New York still your dream?"

"No," I said honestly. "It has its own beauty, but I'd love to be a wedding planner again. Somewhere tropical, ideally, but if I can't swing that, I'll help other couples experience that from afar. Islands truly are magical. Almost as magical as being home." I smiled at Mom, who gave my hand a squeeze. With everything out in the open now, some of the joy Mom had referenced in her phone call swelled in my chest. No secrets, no bad feelings, no underhanded plans. Only love and respect for one another.

"Finish your chicken and then come on a walk with me," Dad said. "There's something I want to tell you." He turned to Mom. "I'll do the dishes when we get back, so hands off."

Mom lifted her palms in surrender, grinning. "Deal."

TWENTY-EIGHT

AFTER DINNER, we headed outside to brave the heat, falling into our usual routine—right turns, all the way around the farm's outer fences. Dirt roads, the occasional whiff of manure, and freshly mowed lawn. I hadn't realized how much I'd missed this.

"I had to bring you out here so your mom wouldn't throttle me later for being right," Dad admitted. "Don't tell her I said this, but I've been a stubborn fool."

"You?" I said with a chuckle. "Never."

"Where do you think your stubborn streak came from?" he asked with a half grin. "Anyway, because of that stubbornness, I missed out on seven years of your life. Not just the day you left, but every day afterward. The cancer may not have taken me from my family, but it broke us all the same. I regret that, Daphne." He held out an elbow.

I blinked rapidly, my eyes suddenly warm, and took his arm as we walked. "Thank you, Dad. You weren't the only one being stubborn. It hurt, being left out, but only because I loved you so much. If the surgery hadn't worked and I was the last to know—I guess it only meant that much less time for me to be prepared. Less time for me to spend with you. But my solution gave me less time with you anyway. I hope you can forgive me."

"No forgiveness necessary. We've both grown up over these seven years. There's something to be said for a fresh start."

A fresh start. Boy, would I love to have one of those with Chase.

"Do you remember the letter?" Dad said slowly, as if unsure whether to bring it up.

I stared at him before understanding dawned. "Of course." I'd been four years old on the day of my adoption. My memories of that day were brushstrokes of moments—saying goodbye to the social worker dropping me off, staring at the new couple grinning at me and feeling shy even though I'd met them before. Hoping they wouldn't hug me even though they clearly wanted to. If I saw the social worker hand them an envelope, I didn't remember it.

Later, on my twelfth birthday, they had presented me with a sealed letter from my biological mom, just as she'd requested. *That* I remembered with perfect clarity.

Dad guided us around a cowpie without blinking. "We worried how you would react to the news of her being in prison, being so young, but the part that concerned us the most was her advice about life."

"*People will always disappoint you,*" I recited. "*Don't trust anyone, even yourself. The only forces you can really trust in this world are fate and destiny, and you'll find them written in the stars.*"

Dad nodded, not surprised that I had the words memorized. "When you grew up constantly trying to call 1-800 numbers to talk to psychics and hid those fortune cards under your mattress—"

"Tarot," I corrected.

"Yeah, those. We just felt like you were clinging to your past and keeping us at a distance. You found other obsessions near the end of high school, but when the cancer diagnosis came . . . "

"You thought I would revert back to all that," I finished for him.

"Exactly. We wanted to keep our daughter during that difficult time without feeling like we had to compete with your birth mom and that strange hold she seemed to have on you. It was selfish, though, and wrong. You have my word that it will never happen again. You deserve to have full reign of your own life without us getting in the way. I know you're a full-grown woman now and it's a little late to be saying it, but I'm saying it all the same."

I fell silent, letting his words sink in. I thought about those moments after fleeing to New York when I'd fallen back on my birth mom's advice to find my way in the world. Clung to coincidences like signs and desperately tried to find meaning in my existence. Found her warning about people being untrustworthy to be true, again and again.

Was this how my birth mom felt when she considered her life? Did she also grasp at stars billions of miles away in an attempt to control the parts of her life that couldn't be controlled?

For the first time in my life, I felt an emotional connection to her, and it made me smile.

"I know you've never understood astrology," I told Dad, "but it got me through a difficult time in my life and I'm grateful for it."

I expected him to argue, but Dad only said, "Then I'm grateful too. You'll have to teach me more about it." He gave me a sideways look. "That is, if you'll be in town for a while."

I sighed. "For the foreseeable future, as I have nowhere else

to go. Not that I wouldn't have come back anyway. It was time."
Not because the universe told me so, but because my heart did.

We walked in silence for a few minutes before Dad spoke again. "You seem sad since you got back. Lose someone you cared about?"

I groaned. "Yes, and it was my own fault."

"You sure it's over?"

Definitely over, with a capital O. "Nobody can put this wreckage back together. Not in a thousand years."

"I see." Dad's voice had an odd note to it. "The thing about wreckage though—it can be cleared and rebuilt." He motioned to the stable in front of us.

My gaze followed his hand and I blinked. Wait a second. The barn looked like it had before, only...not. It stood wider, taller, and newer than I remembered. The paint, once gray and peeling, was now a bright white, and the wide side sported more windows.

"You built a new barn?" I exclaimed.

"First one burned down. Don't worry, we got all the animals out in time, including Rosie." He glanced at me. "I apologize for not letting Mom tell you. We knew you'd worry, and it seemed like you were having such a good time in New York. But I know now that keeping it from you wasn't my call to make."

I stared at the structure in wonder. "It's beautiful."

"Better than before," he said meaningfully. "Just like relationships sometimes."

As I pondered that, Dad pulled the stable door open and motioned for me to enter first. The scent of manure, hay, and sweet oats overwhelmed my senses. I felt like a starving woman facing a Thanksgiving feast, unsure where to start.

Actually, I knew exactly where to start. I hurried to Rosie's stall and started to look over the door, but Rosie's beautiful, hairy muzzle nudged me in the shoulder before I got far. She nickered.

"I have missed you so much," I told her, straightening her ever-messy mane and giving her neck a pat. I drank in the smell of her and sighed. "I'm glad you're still here. Life just isn't the same without you."

Dad dumped a handful of oats into a bucket and handed it over. "Life wasn't the same without you too. But it sounds like you've lived through some tough experiences and come out better for it. Romance is hard, especially."

I snorted. "Yeah, right. You said Mom flipped your world on its head, and you were married within weeks. That isn't how it goes anymore."

"I doubt it's changed much," Dad said. "You just have to know what to look for. Love feels like fate tapping you on the shoulder, telling you to look twice. Like you just found your future in the form of a person."

I shook my head. "Fate and I aren't the best of friends at the moment. I think I'll follow my heart next time. Much more reliable."

Dad squeezed my shoulder. "Nothing a ride through the fields won't solve. Rosie could sure use the exercise."

Suddenly I was a thirteen-year-old again, sneaking to the barn to escape homework and cutting through fields to visit friends. "I need to see Bridget."

"Bet she'll be happy to see you. Just text if you end up staying the night. I know how you two go on."

I threw myself into his arms, which immediately encircled me. "Thanks, Dad."

"You're welcome. Just remember—sometimes a pile of wreckage doesn't mean the end, but clearing ground for a new beginning. We're happy for this new beginning with you."

❤ ❤ ❤ ❤ ❤ ❤

Bridget plunged out her front door before I could even knock, throwing her arms around me. "It's so good to see you! I couldn't believe it when you said you were back. I would have run over right away, but I didn't dare leave Pops alone."

I hugged her back. "I came as soon as I could."

"I know you did." She pulled away and grabbed my shoulders. "Does it feel like stepping back in time?"

"Actually, a lot is different," I admitted. New stores and a gas station I didn't remember. Things like that. "Dad's gray hair was a bit of a shock."

"Your mom has it too, but she colors her hair. Poor Daphne. I know you wouldn't have come home if you'd had any other choice."

"Actually, I would have. It was time."

She grabbed my arm and pulled me toward the doorway. "I'm proud of you. Come in! I have so many questions. Among them, are you staying the night? Are we eating any fortune cookies?"

I made a face. "I think I'm done with fortune cookies for a while."

She closed the door behind us. "The fortune game, then. We need to see who you're marrying."

"I'm marrying whoever I choose. You, on the other hand, are also marrying someone I choose. Let's talk about the eligible bachelors in town. Or outside of it, for that matter."

She laughed. "I do have a couple of prospects I haven't told you about."

"What? I need photos, stat."

A few minutes later, we sat at her parents' giant computer

—which looked like it hadn't budged in seven years—and flipped through social media photos of old friends. While she searched, I caught sight of a browser tucked away on the screen. One of the open windows said Chase's name. "What's that?"

"This? Oh, after you told me that article about Chase was true, I pulled up a few more. I didn't get to read any of them though." Bridget pulled up the window.

The first few articles echoed more about his accusations and court case, but the sixth near the bottom of the page was a newer article. "How about that one?"

She clicked on it, and we began to read.

"Oh, Daphne," Bridget moaned.

I stood there, frozen, staring at the words with a sinking horror in the pit of my stomach.

His aunt's photo was prominently displayed at the top, with the headline CHASE EVERETT CLEARED OF ALL CHARGES.

I skimmed the article and came to an interview with his aunt. Her name wasn't mentioned, but I knew it had to be Carolle.

"Chase did none of those things he was accused of," she'd said. "In fact, I watched Chase try to talk my brother out of adding him to the will. Chase never wanted that money, but now that he has it, he's done nothing but help people. He's donated to charities and scholarship funds and lifted thousands out of poverty. His uncle, my brother, refused to do any of that. I'm glad the judge sees Chase for who he is, because Chase deserves all the happiness in the world."

Bridget finished reading and then turned to me in wonder. "Yes, he does deserve happiness. But you guys are over now, right?"

I chuckled bitterly. "Couldn't be more over. Dead and buried, over."

"But you don't want to be. Does he know that?"

I wasn't sure if he did, not that it mattered. In a moment of guilt, I'd blocked his number from my phone. Hopefully that small gesture would make it slightly easier for him to find happiness with the right woman. The kind he deserved.

I shook my head. "Doesn't matter now."

Bridget stood and pulled me into another hug before putting her hands on my shoulders and looking me square in the eye. "You know what though? I have something important to tell you, so listen carefully."

My eyes felt too warm and blurry. "What's that?"

"You, Daphne, deserve happiness too."

TWENTY-NINE

When I returned home the next morning, Mom had a strange look on her face. "Did you get my text?"

I grabbed my phone and glanced at the screen. "No. Did you send it to the right number?"

She checked her own phone and laughed. "Oh, I sent it to Dad. He must be so confused. He's mowing Mort's lawn across town. Poor man broke his leg last month. Anyway, you had a visitor."

"Who?" Nobody besides Bridget knew I was in town, unless she'd been spreading the word.

"Don't know. Some man. He wouldn't leave his name."

Ty again. The man wouldn't give up. I'd told him about my coming home, so finding my address wouldn't have been that hard. "Where is he now?"

"I told him you were sleeping over at a friend's and he left. Not one for words, that one." She shrugged. "Couldn't see his eyes under his sunglasses, but he seemed mighty handsome."

Sunglasses.

Ty never wore sunglasses.

"Mom," I said breathlessly. "Was he tall, about six feet four inches? Wide shoulders?"

She nodded. "Looked like a football player but with expensive clothes. He seemed disappointed when I told him where you were. I told him you'd be back soon, but he didn't want to stick around. Even when I offered him tea." She seemed surprised by that.

Ty would have stayed. That I knew. There was only one person who fit that description, and I knew exactly what he would have assumed about the "staying over at a friend's house" thing too. "Did he say where he was going?"

"No, but he seemed polite. I was impressed, to be honest. Is he a work friend of yours?"

"How long ago?" I asked impatiently.

She tapped her fingers on her thigh. "Maybe ten minutes ago?"

I bolted out the door before remembering I had no car, and Dad had taken the truck. "Mom!" I shrieked. "I need a vehicle right this second. When will Dad be back?"

"He's only been gone half an hour," she called back.

My mind raced. I could take Rosie to meet my dad and grab the truck, but that would take time I didn't have. The nearest airport was only half an hour away.

I pulled out my phone to call an Uber, then growled in frustration. No available drivers for at least twenty miles. Even if I could convince one to come all the way out here, I'd arrive at the airport too late to find him.

I sprinted to the stable and called to Rosie, who immediately stuck her head over her stall door.

"Sorry, girl," I said, out of breath from running across the field. I grabbed the saddle off its stand and turned to face her. "We aren't done for the day yet."

♥ ♥ ♥ ♥ ♥

Galloping Rosie felt just as I remembered—smooth and fast. At fourteen, she wasn't the youngest of the bunch, but she hadn't forgotten how to run. I chose the dirt road shortcut to protect her legs and cut time, giving her rein to gallop as fast as she wanted. I breathed in the wind and let my hair whip around behind me. The sensation reminded me of the island, except this time, it smelled of home. Hope. Happiness. An opportunity to make everything right, at the very least.

I didn't allow myself to think further than that.

Rosie began to tire before we even reached the frontage road along the highway. Frowning, I pulled her over at the gas station and tied her to a bike rack. A minute later, I emerged from the convenience store with a couple of room-temperature water bottles and a huge dog bowl I'd borrowed from the cashier. Rosie drank happily as I counted the seconds.

It had been twenty-five minutes since Chase's arrival at my home. That meant he could arrive at the airport any minute now, and we were barely a third of the way there.

The foolishness of my situation hit me hard. Did I really intend to ride Rosie all the way to the airport? What would I do once we got there, tie her up in the park-and-ride and run through the airport calling Chase's name? Besides, the frontage road was full of potholes. I didn't want Rosie to get hurt.

I pulled out my phone, but the Uber app said the closest car was still ten minutes away. I requested a ride and then waited, hoping against hope that a driver would accept my request.

Two minutes passed. Three. Four.

The screen went black. Dead.

Crap. I should have charged it at Bridget's last night. Maybe somebody inside would have a charger...or maybe somebody could give me a ride? People hitchhiked to the airport all the time, didn't they?

I headed for the doors again—and then stopped dead in my tracks.

A jet-black Subaru WRX-STI sat parked in one of the gas stalls. A tall man with broad shoulders and aviator sunglasses put the gas dispenser back onto its holster, then opened his car door to climb inside.

"Chase!" I called, running toward him with my hands waving.

The car started, and he pulled onto the main road.

"No!" I sprinted faster, but his speed only increased. Then he was out of sight.

Uttering every curse word I knew, I hurried back to Rosie and fumbled with the knot before swinging astride my trusty steed.

"We've got to catch that car," I told her, and her ears flicked backward. She knew how important this was. Of course she did. The only problem was that I couldn't take Rosie on the busy road. It wouldn't be safe for her or anyone else.

My mind still raced. Chase had his car. That meant he'd driven all the way here from New York. He'd be merging onto the freeway in a few minutes. If we hurried, we could still head him off.

We took the dirt road from earlier but headed north instead of east. A boy drove by on a four-wheeler, watching us hurry past with wide eyes, but I paid him no heed.

This was taking too long. "Come on, girl," I whispered. "Please."

She responded, her ears flicking back and toward the front again as her speed increased.

We slowed to round a turn and took off again, the entire road clear. I could see a black car in the distance. It had to be him. An intersection lay ahead of him, and he looked to be slowing for a red light.

We were going to make it.

Just as we reached the end of the road, a tractor pulled out —pulling a narrow trailer that blocked the entire road.

Rosie didn't hesitate. She leaped over the trailer.

I may have screamed.

We soared like that for a moment, the both of us one and the same as we flew. Even Rosie's hard breaths seemed to sound in slow motion. My scream echoed in the air, reverberating in my ears like the aftershock of a loud concert.

Then Rosie's front hooves hit the ground, jarring me abruptly forward—

And I found myself lying on the ground, staring up at the blue sky with puffy white clouds that looked like giant half-pulled cotton balls.

A face appeared over me. Mr. McCandell. "You all right, little lady? Hey, you're the Porter girl."

I tried to say yes, but my mouth wouldn't obey my command. Suddenly, every inch of my body hurt.

Chase appeared in the sky, his face hovering with the clouds. He tore his sunglasses off, looking positively dumb-founded. "Daphne?"

I lifted my hand to my head. This had to be a concussion. No way would Chase be here otherwise, floating above my face.

"I tried to catch you, but I couldn't fly," I murmured. "You forgot your car."

He glanced at the farmer, who shrugged, and pulled out his phone. "I'm calling an ambulance."

An ambulance. That would be fast. I could definitely catch up to Chase in one of those.

Wait—*Rosie*.

I sat up and looked around before the entire expanse of sky rushed to my head once again. Rosie stood in the middle of a field, happily munching away, still wearing the saddle.

"She's sitting up, son, so probably no spinal injury," the farmer pointed out, then smiled kindly at me. "That was pretty good form you had there. Just make sure to put your weight in your stirrups and lean forward first, then back when you land. Worked for me when Champion and I were jumping, back in the day. You two okay, then?"

I stared at him, willing his words to make sense. If there were two of us, that meant he was either talking to me and Rosie...

Or Chase was actually here.

"Thanks. I'll take her home," Chase said, offering the farmer a friendly wave. Then he looked me up and down once more, as if unconvinced of my health. "That was quite a fall. I saw it from my rearview mirror. Did you hit your head? Where are you hurt?"

My head did hurt, but so did the rest of me. As a test, I managed to get onto my knees and then stand all the way. My legs held firm, if a little shaky. "I'm fine."

He shook his head in wonder. "What were you *doing?*"

I motioned toward his car, parked haphazardly on the sidewalk with one door open and the hazard lights blinking. "Trying to catch you."

He eyed Rosie. "On a horse."

"My dad took the truck, and I don't have a car," I told him. My brain still felt fuzzy, but he needed to hear this. "I'm sorry for lying, but I'm done with that. The truth is, this is who I am." I motioned to the town around me and my wonderful horse and the farmer driving his tractor away while looking back at us over his shoulder. "I'm muddy and jobless and broke. I've been kicked out of my apartment, and now I live with my parents. I make poor decisions when faced with men I never intended to love. Sometimes I think I'm chasing my dreams when I'm actually running from my past. But regardless, I'm absolutely, head over heels, upside down and right-side-up in love with you, Chase Everett."

I heard his breath catch. His Adam's apple bobbed as he swallowed, then he said, "What about Ty?"

"I left him on my doorstep in New York after he offered me Veronica's ring. I don't know where he is now."

Chase's eyebrows rose. "When you left the island without Ty, I didn't allow myself to hope. But then he dumped Veronica and went after you. I assumed I'd find you married."

And he'd driven all the way here anyway. I didn't mean to let it, but hope swelled in my chest. "Why did you come, then?"

He placed a hand on my face and cradled my cheek in his palm. "I've been misunderstood for most of my life. I know how that feels, yet I didn't give you an adequate chance to explain yourself. So when you left Ty behind . . . if there was the tiniest chance you weren't taken, I had to try."

His touch made my brain even foggier. How he did that, throwing my senses into a blender, I would never know. "But you were so angry on the island."

"I was. At first, I thought you'd lied about Veronica, thought even she couldn't stoop that low. When I confronted her, she immediately got defensive and finally admitted that her dad had arranged the whole thing. I think she fled shortly afterward. I barely slept that night. Then a call from the stockholders in New York woke me up. Our stocks had shot up since the day before, setting all kinds of records, and they couldn't figure out why. The resort's website nearly crashed from all the traffic. As of last night, we are completely booked for the next three dry seasons. Tanner's text about making his video was the only clue I had as to why." He chuckled. "It took me far too long to realize you'd arranged that."

"It was the least I could do, and Tanner was more than happy to help. He already had plenty of footage from previous visits."

Chase looked at me in wonder. "After how I treated you, any other person would have stomped away and cursed my name to the sky. But you didn't tank me or my company, Daphne. You saved us like I thought you would—just, in true Daphne form, in a much more creative way than expected." His hand cupped my cheek, his thumb brushing my skin.

"It was just as much for me as you," I told him. "I needed to take responsibility for my own life and choose to take the reins. I had to stop reacting to what other people decided for me and start making the decisions for myself." I gave him a rueful smile. "But I'm confused about something. How did you find me here?" I'd never given him my address, and my parents' information wasn't listed.

"I took the next flight back to New York. I have employee addresses on file so I went straight to your apartment, but your roommates said you'd moved out. So I went to the office after midnight and found it in some of Blythe's records." He made a face. "That woman was so disorganized."

The emergency contact information. *Right.*

"All flights to Arkansas and nearby airports were booked, so I drove through the night to get here. And when your mom said you were staying over..."

"At a *girl*friend's house," I finished for him. "My best friend from high school. Ty isn't from here, and he isn't a part of my life any longer. I'm not sure why he was ever in my life to begin with. Maybe I didn't believe I deserved anything better."

Chase stood just inches away now, his voice gruff. "And what do you believe now?"

"That this is all a dream. That you're not really here, and I'll wake up and find myself plastered on a dirt road."

He chuckled and tenderly wiped a wayward hair out of my face, sweeping it behind my ear. "I mean, about us."

I let my face drop, staring at my feet. "I *believe* I said I'm in love with you, and you didn't say anything back."

A moment passed. Then his thumb hooked beneath my chin and lifted my face to look upward at his. "I didn't want to say goodbye," he drawled. "And now that you're in my arms again, I'm not saying goodbye to you. Not now, not ever. Now, I won't say you're mine, because that's up to you. But darlin', I am utterly and completely yours."

I was a puddle on the ground. More melted than a puddle —like groundwater. Completely and utterly helpless at the sincerity I saw in his eyes.

"Look," I said. "I know you said you wouldn't kiss me without permission, but—"

He brought my face to his and kissed me so fiercely I felt my feet leave the ground and the cottony clouds encircle us in fuzzy, glorious happiness.

A few more moments, and we pulled away, breathless.

"What were we talking about again?" I managed.

"You were taking me home to meet your parents," he said.

"Right. And you were staying overnight while we worked out travel details."

He cocked his head. "Travel details?"

I shrugged. "We have a company to save, right? Wedding season isn't over. Your island needs you."

"It needs us," he corrected.

I couldn't love that more. I felt dizzy at the thought, my

body barely able to contain its giddy happiness. "There's only one little problem."

"What's that?"

I pointed at my horse, who had trotted off to join a herd of cows in the pasture. "I don't think she'll fit in your car."

We laughed, and everything was exactly as it should be.

THIRTY

Turns out I did see Ty again.

That autumn, after a glorious summer full of each other, we returned to Manhattan triumphant. Chase's company had managed to turn a profit and we were scheduled out for at least four full dry seasons with a long waiting list. Some of the islanders even wanted to add on to the resort, extending it by another fifty rooms. Chase wouldn't hear of it.

As we walked through Four Seasons Park one cool fall evening, hand-in-hand, Chase stopped in his tracks. "Is that...?"

I peered ahead of us, where a couple stood arguing. I would know that man anywhere. "Yep."

"—don't know what you're talking about," Ty was saying.

"You're telling me I don't know about my own life?" a woman shouted at him. It definitely wasn't Veronica. This woman seemed about ten years younger, barely twenty. She stood on the grass with her arms folded, her face turned away.

"I'm saying your life would go better if you listened to me," Ty said, standing stubbornly on the sidewalk. "I know all about this stuff." Then he froze, finally seeing us on the path, and his shoulders tensed.

I lifted a hand to wave. "Hello, Ty."

The girl perked up and hurried over. "Chase Everett! I didn't think you went on walks. I figured you had limos to take you everywhere."

"I've never ridden in a limo," Chase admitted. "And this is a pleasant evening walk with the woman I love." He watched Ty as he finished.

Ty's face went even redder.

The girl gasped and hurried to me, lifting my hand. "What a pretty ring! Are you guys engaged?"

"We haven't told anybody yet," I said with a smile, "but yes." I held my hand up so she could admire it. I shouldn't have, but I took great pleasure in seeing Ty's sputtering behind her.

"Simple yet elegant," the girl cooed. "I've never seen anything like it, but it's perfect."

"Thank you." I couldn't help but grin along with her. The gold band tapered daintily toward the stone, which was a beautiful blue color, a special type found only in a specific mine off the coast of Costa Rica. I couldn't have asked for anything better.

"I would have expected it to be bigger," Ty grumbled.

"That stone is worth more than an entire floor of condos in the city," Chase said lightly, and his hand tightened on my elbow as he nudged us past them. "Nice to see you both."

I felt both their eyes on my back as we walked around them and started for the park's entrance. I leaned into Chase and he wrapped his arm around my waist while we walked.

"That was surprisingly fulfilling," he said.

"I was thinking the same thing."

When we were alone again, he pulled me around in front

of him and kissed me deeply. "So, soon-to-be-Mrs. Everett, have you decided where you want the ceremony to take place? I know how much you love New York, but then Rosie couldn't take part, and that just doesn't seem right after she worked so hard to bring us together."

"It doesn't, but she wouldn't enjoy riding an airplane to the island, either, so that's probably a no-go."

"She would hate the plane ride. It'll have to be a ship." His smile widened. "Hold on. You do want to get married on the island?"

I grinned. "Duh. But we have to be barefoot, or the deal's off. Everyone. The entire wedding party. And half should be wearing swimsuits."

"I wouldn't complain about tying the knot with you wearing yours," he said, breaking into a wicked grin.

"The guests, silly. My mom won't rest until she's covered me in six miles of cloth and a homemade wedding dress in the style of forty years ago."

"I'm sure you'll be beautiful. We'll have the entire island take part." He sobered, all business now. "There's lots to be done. We need to set the date and start making the arrangements with the caterer, since that's the part that tends to go awry—"

"If only you were marrying a wedding planner who could take care of these details," I said pointedly. I'd taken back over my role upon returning to the island. With such a long client list these days, I'd also hired a few more assistants to help.

"Touché. I'll let you worry about that. In the meantime, I have a few other details to take care of. The honeymoon, for example."

"So mysterious." I threw my arms around his neck again. "Many couples travel to islands for their honeymoons, but we already have one of those. You don't want to stay on Isle de Pura Vida?"

"Not when I have something better."

"Better? Not possible."

He chuckled, low and deep. "Well, *little lady*," he drawled. "I guess you'll just have to trust me."

EPILOGUE

TANNER

I TRIED. I really did. But helping out a friend in need with a quick travel video was one thing...and attending his wedding was entirely another.

I usually avoided weddings whenever possible. Talk about cheesy awkwardness. Melting, stinking, uncomfortable cheese bars galore. The couple are smiling, the guests are smiling, and all the decorations look the same from one ceremony to the next—white gauze everywhere and twinkly lights that remind me of a six-year-old's bedroom.

Although I had to admit that they'd chosen the perfect place for the ceremony, with its gorgeous ocean backdrop. And the barefoot thing was new. I couldn't complain about the free vacation either. My YouTube channel was doing better than ever, so I could have afforded the resort fee, but Chase insisted on footing the bill.

Now, looking around, I realized that he'd probably paid for all forty of the attendees sitting with me in the audience. I did the math and nearly whistled, long and slow. Yep, Chase had come a long way since our high school grad days of scrawniness and searching for life's meaning in the adventurous rainforests of Costa Rica.

The violinist stopped playing, took a gulp from her water bottle, and began again. She'd been playing the same six songs over and over for nearly an hour now. The officiator—the governor of this little island—stood in his best suit, calm as anything, but the other guests looked as confused as I felt. Where were the bride and groom?

A squeal sounded behind us, and I turned in my seat along with the others. Down the beach, Daphne jumped up and down next to the ugliest horse I'd ever seen before throwing her arms around Chase. Then she led the horse toward us. Would this be a horseback wedding? More drippy, mind-numbing cheese.

But no. She walked the horse right up to me, tied it onto the chair next to mine, gave my shoulder a pat, and bounded into the trees and out of sight.

Huh. Maybe not such a typical wedding after all.

I gave the horse a sideways glance and it snorted, spraying me with every germ known to man and probably horses too.

"Thanks a lot," I muttered.

The horse actually nodded.

Chase strode to the front, removed his shoes, and nodded to the violinist, who switched songs mid-note to Pachabel's Canon in D. How original.

A rustle went through the crowd as we stood. Daphne had appeared in the trees again, yet we were supposed to pretend like we hadn't just seen her sprinting across the sand with her gown hiked to her knees. Clearly somebody had cleaned her up a bit, though, because her curls lay close to her face once again.

The horse tried to pull away from the chair as if to go to her.

"Whoa, Nellie," I whispered.

Daphne walked slowly down the aisle, wearing a quiet smile. She seemed a little wild but very genuine—not at all the reserved, high-bred bride I'd imagined for Chase. He wore an even wider smile, as if it were he, not her, who'd scored a huge win today. I would support marriage to any woman who could make my ever-somber friend smile like that.

About ten years later, she finally reached the front and the officiator started speaking in broken English.

I felt something on my hair and swatted it away. Not a bug. A horse's muzzle.

"It's hair, not hay," I muttered to the animal.

The ceremony went beautifully until the very end, when it all happened in slow motion.

The horse decided it was done waiting and started walking toward the front, at which moment I realized too late that these chairs were all linked together. My chair tipped and dumped me right into the sand.

I leaped to my feet and grabbed the horse's leash, or whatever it's called, to turn it around in the tight aisle. Then I led it to the back again as the audience laughed. Why Daphne had made me the official horse-sitter, I didn't know, but I could at least keep the thing away from the main event for another minute or two.

The couple finally kissed and everyone stood and cheered. I threw up a half-hearted fist as I stood there, keeping the leash taut and the horse just behind my shoulder.

Which it really didn't want to do, apparently, because it chose that moment to whinny—right next to my ear.

I yelped and held my poor ear, which now rang like a small-town church on Christmas Day. The audience laughed even harder, including Chase and Daphne.

"Let her go," Daphne said, reaching out her arms like the horse was an infant.

I tossed the leash over the horse's neck and gave her butt a pat. "Go see your mommy."

The horse trotted across the sand and down the aisle, stumbling a bit on the light fabric rug before shoving her way between the newly wedded couple, almost defensively, as if to make it clear who Daphne really belonged to.

The audience practically rolled now. I just wiped horse spit off my sleeve.

"The Everett family," the officiator called, and everyone cheered.

Okay, not so bad for a wedding. At least the horse had made things interesting.

❤ ❤ ❤ ❤ ❤

"Now we know who to leave Rosie with while we're gone," Daphne said at the reception that evening, smiling apologetically. "She likes you, Tanner."

"Yeah. Likes me for breakfast."

Chase chuckled as a woman came over and pulled Daphne away for a moment, leaving Chase and me alone.

"She seems like an intriguing woman," I told him.

Chase nodded. "Certainly keeps me guessing. I'm pretty sure this is the part where I tell you it's your turn."

"Oh, I'm sure some lucky turd will earn that privilege at the garter toss."

"Garter or not, there's a woman in your future. Better this time. Let's hope she doesn't like horses though. I don't think they're quite your thing." He elbowed me in the side.

"*She* won't, because *she* doesn't exist. I'm free as a bird." I leaned over to whisper. "Hey, where could you two be going tonight that's better than here? You don't have to tell me, but tell me anyway."

Chase grinned. The guy looked so unbelievably happy, I wanted to puke. "Thanks to your video and the huge surge in stocks, I bought another island just north of here. Equally beautiful, but far more secluded with only a single bungalow. I named it after her."

The cheesiest thing I'd heard all night. "Smart. I'm happy for you, man. Really."

"You know I'll be there when your big day comes. Pretty sure that'll be sooner than later. Don't skip the garter throw, though, just in case." Chase slapped me on the back and walked over to join Daphne.

I did skip the garter toss. I even left early and wandered the island with bare feet, gazing up at a sky full of incredible stars. But it wasn't until the next morning at the airport that I really let Chase's words sink in.

He didn't understand. I'd done the dating thing, nearly gotten married to the woman of my dreams. Even sent Chase a wedding announcement.

Turned out those dreams were actually a nightmare.

Later I found my seat on the plane and gazed out the tiny window at Chase's island. I knew better than anyone else what I wanted in life, and it wasn't what Chase thought I needed. Or my mom, or my brother, or anyone else.

I'd never be rich enough to own an island, but I could direct my own life. And that seemed really nice right now, after years of captivity with the wrong woman.

Nope, Tanner Carmichael was a free man, traveling wherever and whenever he wanted. I would show Chase and everyone else that I could be single forever and still be happy. Bachelor life suited me.

They'd see. Every last one of them.

Continue reading Tanner's story in JUST CAN'T FALL FOR THE ENEMY or read on for a sneak peek now!

SASHA HART

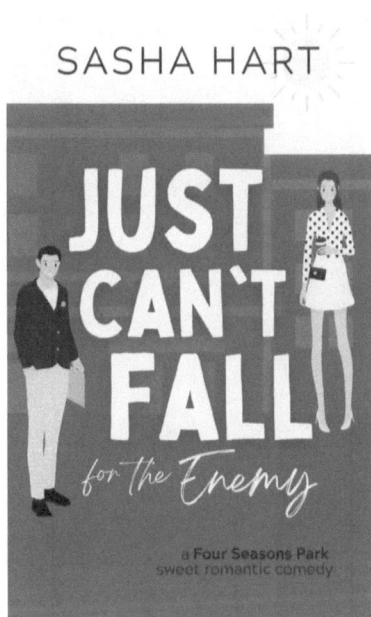

SNEAK PEEK: JUST CAN'T FALL FOR THE ENEMY

Sophie

I stared at the man sitting in front of me—all 150 pounds of high breeding and expensive tailored shirt of him. He didn't stare back as he was currently too busy judging every inch of the restaurant with a frown. "So," he began, "why did you want to meet here again?"

It's the nicest restaurant in town. I didn't say it and prided myself on not throwing the entire basket of garlic bread at his face, tugging at the sleeve of my nicest blouse instead. "It's a good central meeting place. You're staying at the hotel, right?"

"If you can call it that." He sniffed. "What an . . . *interesting* place to live."

I felt my body tense and told myself to calm down. Huckleberry Creek, Montana, was the most charming small town in existence. The fact that he couldn't see it only proved this entire night—and the earlier twenty minutes spent straightening my hair—would be a waste of time. "You don't like small towns?"

He wrinkled his nose at a family with several children sitting nearby, all in worn yet clean clothes. "Let's just say these aren't my people. Obviously my mother has never set foot here, or she would have flown you to Chicago to meet me instead." His fork hovered over his plate of pasta, drawing my eye to a pair of cuff links. *Cuff links.*

I wouldn't have gone to Chicago for a date with a rich prince, let alone the whiny son of a senator. I'd only agreed to this blind date to make Grammy happy. Apparently, she and the senator lady were friends. Staring at this man and his permanent pout, I couldn't imagine why. His collar fell slightly open, just casual enough for the occasion yet perfectly fitted like a politician's speech outfit. Made sense, considering who his mother was. Everything about his appearance screamed, "Eligible and desirable man in search of a doting wife." Why he assumed me a candidate was beyond me.

"So, anyway," he said again. "Let's get on with it. What do you think a wife's role is in our society?"

I didn't ask what we were getting on *with*. He'd stared at his lap as he asked the question, just as with the last two oddly formal questions. He'd ordered for me against my insistence otherwise, claiming the online reviews praised this spaghetti. He forgot I'd grown up in this town. I knew every inch of it, including who probably made this and every detail about the server who brought it to our table. I'd even attended the opening of Alice's Italy House, for goodness' sake. The only reason a man would insist on ordering spaghetti for a woman was to test her breeding.

Well, two could play that game.

I shoveled a huge bite into my mouth, making sure one of

the noodles hung over my bottom lip, and talked around the food. "Wives should live the same way as their husbands, doing whatever they want." I slurped the noodle into my mouth as messily as possible.

He frowned. "Even a senator's wife?"

"Especially a senator's wife. Sounds like a very lonely place to be if you ask me." I picked up the glass of ice water, brought it to my mouth, and slurped loudly.

He flinched and fixed his gaze on his lap again. "Uh, okay. Moving on. I wondered if you want children and, if so, how many?"

Yep. Definitely reading off a list. Now I was curious. Did he or his mother write it?

I took another bite, bigger this time. "Fourteen," I said with a full mouth. "Two to do the yard work, ten to do the cooking, and three for laundry. Then I can watch more episodes of *Abandoned on an Island*. Oh, and five dogs."

His eyes positively bugged now. "I . . . fourteen?"

"And five dogs," I repeated. "One pit bull, one Great Dane, one boxer, a poodle mix, and a Chihuahua."

"But pit bulls are dangerous."

A giggle nearly erupted from my cramping stomach—I hated spaghetti—but I contained it barely in time. "Not true. I have one, and he's never tried to eat a child. He did take a chunk out of a date's leg once, but we got him to the hospital in plenty of time. Oh, and I forgot the cats. I want to run a cat rescue with at least twenty."

"Stray cats?"

"The strayest of all strays."

I'd gone too far. His eyes narrowed in suspicion. "I want two children, a boy and a girl. No pets."

"Good for you." I also thought two was the perfect number,

but I'd fake a heart attack before I admitted that to Mr. Perfect Teeth.

His mouth tightened in displeasure, and he looked down at his lap once more. "What instruments do you play?"

Seriously?

I shoved another bite in and chewed it with my mouth open, being sure to roll it around for good measure. His eyes widened as he stared at the pasta hanging half in, half out.

"I have a harmonica," I said, though it didn't sound like English. "Oh! And a recorder, from third grade."

"Mm-hmm." His shoulders lifted and fell again as if he heaved a great internal sigh. I wanted to pump my fists in victory.

"Have you ever been on TV?" he asked.

That one was easy. "Heavens, no. Nor do I ever want to be. I like my privacy, thank you very much."

His eyes flashed with something I couldn't read. "Shame. You have the figure for it."

He was honestly flirting with me right now? I could just walk out, but then he would have won. This date needed to end, and I needed him to be the first to surrender.

Time for drastic measures. Embarrassing ones.

I picked up my fork and scooped as much spaghetti as it would hold. When the fork was full, I lifted my knife and used it to support the pasta that remained, letting the giant spaghetti nest hover inches from my mouth.

The man's eyes went round.

I smirked and opened my mouth as far as it would go, shoving it all inside at once. The noodles dribbled down to my neck, splattering marinara all over my shirt and, to my satisfaction, one of his pristine cuff links. "Mmm," I moaned around the food. "So goot."

My stomach lurched, but it was worth it to see him lean

back as if trying to put more distance between us, pure horror written across his face.

I eyed his plate. "Ah ooh going to eah that?"

He went green as I brought his plate closer and started to dig in. Then I grabbed my glass, which he'd filled to the brim—test number two and the first thing that tipped me off to his little test—and sipped it as loudly as I could, emitting a sickly slurping noise. A little girl giggled from the booth behind me. Most of the restaurant had gone quiet, I now realized, and watched with huge grins. They weren't this man's people, but they were most certainly mine—and they knew I had their backs tonight.

He closed his eyes and gritted his teeth. "H-have you ever been to a black-tie event?"

He was *still here*. How far would he make me take this? I thought quickly. "Only once, but not as a guest."

His shoulders tensed. "A waiter?"

"No, no. I was the entertainment." I picked up my glass, chugged half of it, and summoned my high school belching skills. It came at will—an eight out of ten but still acceptable.

The entire restaurant went still, the only movement coming from the man sitting behind my date, facing the other way in his booth. His shoulders began to bounce, his hand to his mouth to contain his laughter.

I wiped my mouth off and sighed loudly. "What do you think? Dessert?"

"I have to go." My date bolted, his face as green as the bush outside our window. The bell dinged as the glass door slammed shut behind him.

The restaurant's occupants began to roar with laughter. The little family's father came over to slap me on the back. "Best shutdown I've ever seen, Sophie. They'll be talking about this for years."

"To Sophie," a woman said, raising her glass of Diet Coke.

Most of the room lifted their glasses to the ceiling, including the little girl with her juice box. "To Sophie."

I stood and gave a little curtsy. "Enjoy your night, everyone. I don't think we'll be seeing him again."

As the father returned to his seat and the room resumed conversation, I let myself relax.

You could have just walked out, I chided myself. That would have been the more mature thing to do. But stalking out of a bad date didn't have the same . . . pizazz as driving him dramatically from town. And this had been far worse than a bad date. Drastic measures, indeed.

The man in the next booth stood, turned around, and gave a slow clap. "Well done."

Oh no.

I swallowed. This man was everything my date wasn't—casual, with short, dark-brown hair styled in a messy yet trendy way; comfortable jeans; and an open plaid shirt with a white undershirt that emphasized his strong build. A light, well-trimmed layer of stubble covered his chin. He wore sunglasses despite the setting sun outside. Something about him seemed oddly familiar.

"Thank you," I said, still standing awkwardly by the messy table. My stomach suddenly rumbled, begging to empty itself of the contents I'd just inhaled. I had thirty seconds to a minute, tops. I found a fifty-dollar bill in my purse and tossed it next to my plate, hoping it would be enough. I'd have to call Alice tomorrow and apologize for tonight's scene.

"Do you always drive obnoxious dates off in such an entertaining way?" the attractive stranger asked, dropping a wad of cash onto his own table.

Uh-uh. The handsome stranger was not following me out,

not now. Even his voice seemed familiar somehow. Where had I met him before?

"Only in Italian restaurants," I said. "He should have chosen Chinese."

He frowned. "Are you all right? You don't look well."

My stomach turned over again. "Excuse me," I said, sprinting for the restroom, which was, thankfully, unlocked. I heard his chuckle even through the door.

When I emerged ten minutes later, he stood where I'd left him. Lovely. He handed me my fifty back and closed my hand around it, his touch electrifying my entire arm. "You shouldn't have to pay for that jerk. Consider this my apology for the less-mannered of my gender. What's your name?"

I cleared my throat, relieved I'd been able to find some mint gum in my purse, but all that came to mind was a replay of tonight's events. The fourteen children and cats and dogs and the spaghetti . . . curse that limp pasta to the sky. I wouldn't be eating pasta again for a very long time. And the belch—*that* would be very hard to explain away. My traitorous face flamed again.

"Think of me as the dinner entertainment," I said, shoving the crumpled bill back at him. "You shouldn't have to pay for him either. Believe me, it was a pleasure to drive him from my town. Men like that don't belong here."

"Oh? Are you the town's designated protector?"

I thought about my young friend, Nate, and felt my determination surge. "Something like that."

He rejected the offering, shaking his head. "Please. It's the least I can do." He looked me up and down, making the heat in my cheeks creep down my neck. I'd scrubbed at the spaghetti sauce on my blouse, but patches of pink stubbornly remained. What kind of impression had I given him and everyone else in this room? And yet . . . he now wore a look of approval. Maybe even admiration. Was that a hint of red on his own neck?

An urge for my bed and a pint of Mintee's ice cream overcame me. "Thank you, then. Glad you enjoyed the show." I brushed past him to the parking lot and my car. I'd parked near the back, of course, impossibly far away.

The man actually followed me. "Question. If a guy met you at a Chinese restaurant, would he have a better chance?"

No, no, *no*. This was not happening. Not with spaghetti-sauce stains and probably puke on my blouse.

My car beeped as I hit the button on my key fob, and I yanked the door open to slide in. Then I gave him a tight smile. "I don't know that I'll be going on any more dates for a while, thank you." *Or eating dinner again, for that matter.*

"Wait." His voice held an edge of surprise. "You really won't tell me your name?"

After that scene? Not a chance. Besides, he was obviously passing through. With any luck, I'd never see him again. "Have a good night."

He unlocked his own car—an expensive red coupe, of course—and stood there watching me with little expression as I drove away.

CHAPTER 2

TANNER

A light chill hung in the autumn air as I watched the woman go.

What was that about?

I stood next to my car longer than I should, half hoping she would come back, but her taillights disappeared in the distance. I recalled her little show inside and chuckled again. She'd put her date in his place without a single rude word. Impressive, especially since the guy acted like we were still living in the 1950s and women were expected to push out babies and have dinner on the table by five. I'd had half a mind to say something, but it hadn't been necessary.

Most of the gorgeous ones would rather die than put on a performance like that. What confidence. And I didn't even know her name.

A crowd gathered at the restaurant window, some with hands cupped to see better. Clearly, a few of the restaurant-goers had figured out who I was. My cue to leave. I folded my six-foot frame into my fusion-red Tesla. My car stood out in this town, no doubt. But that was part of the reason I bought it. A gift for myself after I received my first $100,000 paycheck. There had been many of those since, all piling up in my checking account, waiting for the day I knew what to do with them. It wasn't like a guy who'd spent the past four years traveling needed a mansion or a garage full of cars.

Maybe an apartment, though. Someplace to call home. And companionship that didn't require autographs and selfies at every turn. My dating life was, unfortunately, choppy and disconnected these days—the product of a career that kept me on the move. Probably better that the woman hadn't given me the time of day.

This is the life you chose, I reminded myself. *Most people would kill for the money you're making.*

As I drove down Main Street, I couldn't help but admire its charm. On the left was a park filled with benches, walkways, and loads of enormous trees that looked even older than the town. Strings of lights gave it a romantic air with the darkening sky above. On the far side of the park stood a gazebo beneath which sat a quartet of musicians in casual dress, as if they'd spontaneously put this together. The song that floated on the air sounded slightly twangy, like an old country ballad. An older couple danced on the grass below. With its tree-lined streets and the leaves turning brilliant shades of red, yellow, and orange, Huckleberry Creek was practically a movie set.

And I would be the first YouTuber to feature it.

A wave of nostalgia rushed through my veins. A long time ago, I'd had different plans—college, followed by a steady job. Then a friend's move and invitation for me to join him in Costa

Rica became the perfect opportunity to ditch my local community college for a different kind of adventure. I started my travel channel—not the boring, informational kind but a show revealing the lesser-known tourist gold of various destinations. Before long, brands asked me to promote their stuff in exchange for hefty paychecks. Now, after only a few years of work, my channel had nearly twenty million followers.

It had become my career whether I liked it or not. Mostly I liked it. I'd even asked my assistant, Jill, to reach out to another popular YouTuber star, Guy Hadley, to see if he wanted to collaborate. So far, he hadn't given me a glance, and I didn't blame him. He was the most popular YouTuber on the planet with hundreds of millions of subscribers. He'd even appeared in a movie recently. Hooking him into a collaboration would launch my channel into the stratosphere. Success like that would be impossible for anyone to ignore, including my deadbeat Dad who was currently who-knew-where.

I flung the thought away in distaste. My career had nothing to do with him. Or my life, for that matter.

"Welcome to Huckleberry Creek," I began, speaking into my phone. "Small Town Central, USA. Population 1,100. Or maybe five hundred if you don't count the stray dogs. My first impression is that—"

A shadow appeared on the road.

I slammed on my brakes just in time. A doe stood there, ready to spring, watching me curiously.

I uttered a curse under my breath. "Where did you come from?" Her ears flicked back and forth as if she heard me, though she didn't move an inch. Apparently she didn't want me returning to my hotel anytime soon.

"You were this close to becoming deer jerky, lady dude," I told her, holding up my thumb and index finger to indicate an inch, though the animal didn't seem to care. She stared at me for a long moment before continuing on her way, heading for the shops across the street like she had a bag of cash and time to spare. I ended the recording and blew out a breath to steady my nerves. I would delete that last clip and start again tomorrow. Thoughts of the woman at the restaurant filled my mind, making it impossible to think about my channel right now. The way her brown eyes flashed when she spoke and the twinkle in them had me wishing I'd asked her out rather than just hinting at it. But then, I would only be here for six days.

The last thing I needed was another person to say goodbye to.

Someone behind me honked, and I flinched, checking my rearview mirror. The deer was long gone, and I looked like a doofus hanging out in the middle of the road. I stuck my hand out the window and waved. "Sorry," I called out and took my foot off the brake.

The second I arrived at the hotel and plopped onto the hard bed, my phone rang. "Tanner Carmichael," I said without bothering to glance at the screen. My focus was on the moth fluttering around on the ceiling. How did that get in? Probably the window. A terrible draft blew through from the ill-fitted frame, which looked like it had been installed in the 1800s.

"You're not going to believe this," Jill said.

My pulse quickened at hearing my assistant's voice. She must have heard back from Guy Hadley. "Try me."

"He's interested." There was a note of excitement to her voice but also an edge of hesitation.

I stamped down the thrill inside at her news. "But?"

"He likes your stuff, but he wants to see more than just places and history. He wants a video that feels more personal. Something with drama and authenticity."

I was confused, but Jill went on. "He wants something that

features the people within the city—their stories and why they chose to live there and what it's really like."

"So he wants me to completely change my content." My first response was to get angry. Who did this guy think he was? I had twenty million followers. That wasn't a number to joke about, especially since gaining subscribers was becoming much more difficult these days. Of course, there were several influencers who had more than I did. A lot more. But most didn't even come close to my numbers.

Jill paused. "Maybe not permanently. I think one solid episode would do the trick."

My pride still smarted at Guy's critique. I wasn't sure I wanted to change anything, let alone the very heart of my channel.

"I'll call you back," I said and hung up.

I wasn't a diva and never had been. Brands had turned me down before, and that was fine. But this was different. I really wanted to collaborate with Guy. Or at least I needed him if I wanted to continue to grow my business. And I did—more than anything. I couldn't say why, but the more success I had, the more I craved. Bigger, better. Higher. That hunger kept me going on the hard and lonely days. Besides, my videos were art, each one feeding into the next, like I was telling the story of the location for my viewers.

Grumbling my frustration, I tucked my phone into my back pocket and hopped onto my computer to do a little research on Huckleberry Creek. Not much to find. It was the one problem with randomly choosing my locations on a map in front of millions of people—I had no idea what I would find there, if anything.

Clearly, I wouldn't be compiling a script based on what I found online. I needed to recruit a local to help, someone who knew the town well and loved it fiercely. Someone acquainted with every single one of those 1,100 people who made their lives in Huckleberry Creek. Some well-respected person who knew their stories.

Someone like the woman from the restaurant.

I thought for a long moment, took out my phone, and texted Jill.

I'm in.

Continue reading Sophie & Tanner's story in
Just Can't Fall for the Enemy now or visit SashaHart.com to
bundle and save 40% on the entire series!

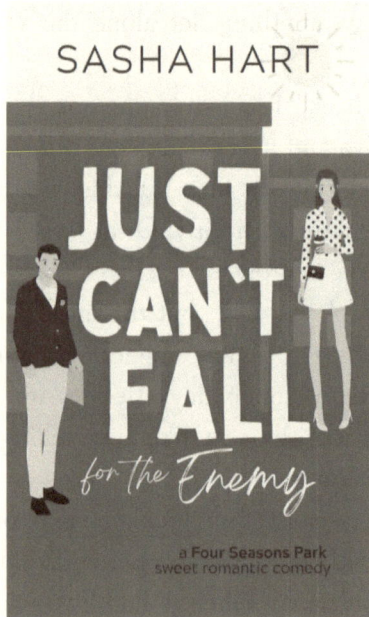

FOUR SEASONS PARK SWEET ROMANTIC COMEDIES

Four couples. Four seasons.
One park to (hilariously) match them all.

FOUR SEASONS PARK by Sasha Hart

Don't miss a single Four Seasons Park romcom! Get the entire series and TWO FREE bonus shorts for 40% off now on Sasha Hart.com.

Before You Go

Don't forget
to leave
a review!
(Thank you!)

♥ ♥ ♥ ♥ ♥ ♥

ABOUT THE AUTHOR

SASHA HART writes sweet romantic comedies that remind her of her all-time favorite movies--which include pretty much anything starring Sandra Bullock, Meg Ryan, or Julia Roberts. She's also obsessed with modern authors like Jenny Han, Sarah J. Maas, Sabaa Tahir and pretty much any author who can give her all the feels. Besides romantic movies and books, she also loves arguing about which is the best Pride & Prejudice adaptation. (Collin Firth, all the way.) She can usually be found in her office, helping characters find their swoony happily ever afters.

Made in United States
Troutdale, OR
05/29/2024